JOAN MAKES HISTORY

By the same author

Bearded Ladies
Lilian's Story
Dreamhouse

JOAN MAKES HISTORY

Kate Grenville

British American Publishing

Copyright 1988 by Kate Grenville
All rights reserved
including the right of reproduction
in whole or in part in any form
First published in Australia by
University of Queensland Press
American edition first published in 1988 by
British American Publishing
3 Cornell Road
Latham, NY 12110
Manufactured in the United States of America

93 92 91 90 89 5 4 3 2

Library of Congress Cataloging in Publication Data

Grenville, Kate, 1950—
Joan makes history / Kate Grenville
p. cm.
ISBN 0-945167-09-1
I. Title.
PR9619.3.G73J63   1988
823—dc19   88-23679
CIP

for Bruce

PROLOGUE

IN the beginning was nothing much. Vague things swirled and whirled, impulses grouped and dissolved, light came and went. It was a fluke, or a leap of faith: but there it was all at once, the first atom, and everything else was just a matter of time.

Imagine the stars burning their hearts out in brand-new galaxies! Imagine the time when bundles of hot gas decided to draw together and be Mars or Earth! Imagine the first rain sizzling down on the first hot rocks, and starting the business of the land and the sea! What aeons of racket there were, of magma squirting up and lava gushing out: what tumult as the globe heated, froze, cracked, drowned: as rock wore away to sand that ebbed and flowed on the floors of warm seas. What convulsions there were, as the bottom of the sea became the top of a surprised mountain steaming in the sun and melting away again, until at last it formed the shapes of Africa and Iceland and the Great South Land!

Imagine dew forming, sun scorching, winds whipping: lichen grasping the side of a rock: grass sprouting and dying, small flowers holding their faces up to the sun. Imagine saplings thickening, putting forth leaves and dropping them off: imagine them swelling at last beyond the strength of the roots and crashing back down to the ground, and from their ruin new trees springing.

Consider the extravagant excess of nature, providing every different bit of earth with its particular kind of life: with Pale Prickly Moses, with the Leafless Milkwort, with the Spoonleaf Sundew: with the Gregarious Stick Insect, with the Sugar Ant, with the Small Green-Banded Blue Butterfly, with the Pie-Dish Beetle, with the Yellow Monday Cicada and the Shining Swift Moth: with the Yellow-Bellied Black Snake, the Sulphur-Crested White Cockatoo, the Frill-Necked Lizard: with the Crest-Tailed Pouched Mouse as well as the Flat-Headed Pouched Mouse: what an unnecessary prodigality of supply!

Imagine, too, those formless jellies from which they say we come: something—what was it?—made them desire history, clustering together and becoming particular: *You be skin, I will be legs.* What a journey it was, from the trilobite, the graptolite, the pterygotus, to the pterodactyl, the brontosaurus, the tyrannosaurus rex! Things with teeth where their ears should have been, things with four mouths and seven feet, things with eggs the size of houses and tongues as long as tree-trunks!

They trundled and hopped, slithered and leaped, swam, flapped and waddled, and after them came the humans who left footprints in the dust. So many births: imagine them, born every second of every day, year after year: now, and now, and now, and now, just now there are three, four, five new humans in the world, I cannot speak quickly enough to outstrip them. They are pink, brown, or yellow, angry or solemn, arching in a midwife's hands or staring around in a knowing way: bursting forth with a roar, or being lifted astonished out of cut flesh. They suck blindly at nipples, they whimper or crow, they lie in possum-skin rugs or a proud father's arms. Imagine them in their millions, all driven by the same few urgent

4

promptings: to suck, to grasp, to kick, and at last to smile, and with that smile to begin their public life.

So many lives! Being explorers or prisoners of the Crown, hairdressers or tree-choppers, washerwomen or judges, ladies of leisure or bareback riders, photographers or mothers or mayoresses.

I, Joan, have been all these things. I am known to my unimaginative friends simply as Joan, born when this century was new, and now a wife, a mother, and a grandmother: Joan who has cooked dinners, washed socks, and swept floors while history happened elsewhere. What my friends do not know is that I am also every woman who has ever drawn breath: there has been a Joan cooking, washing, and sweeping through every event of history, although she has not been mentioned in the books until now.

Allow me to introduce myself: Joan, a woman as plain as a plate, and devoid of bust, a grandmother you would pass on the street without a glance. Allow me also to acquaint you with a small selection of those other Joans, those who made the history of this land.

I will begin in the beginning, with myself.

JOAN

MY conception: It was not night, no, Europeans have no shame and do not trouble to wait, as we do, until dark for lust. It was the middle of a hot afternoon in the first year of the century, with the sun blazing down outside on planks steaming and adding their salt dampness to air that was already too thick to breathe. It was afternoon, and the rhythm of a thin woman and a thick balding man was attuned, after so many months, to the restless rocking and shifting of the boat under the mattress—oh, that mattress and its manifold rustlings!—on which they coupled.

This was a ship built to transport many in cheapness rather than a few in luxury. It was a mean and cramped ship, a ship of tiny airless cabins with peeling walls, cracked ceilings, and dripping pipes in the corners that conveyed other people's plumbing with a rush and rattle late at night.

Those seedy cabins had occasionally heard the roiling and difficult syllables, the guttural hawkings and strange sibilances of some of Europe's lesser-known languages, and had echoed even more to the ingenious obscenities and sly rude wit of many folk from Lambeth, Bow, and Cheapside. They had echoed to the sighs of gentlewomen

9

in reduced circumstances, weeping into embroidered lawn and hankering for home: weeping, but knowing that their chance of husband and hearth, livelihood and life worth living would not be found in the genteel squalor of some seedy out-of-season Brighton boarding house, but here, in this savage new land that wanted everyone: carpenters, cooks, governesses, dentists, and hopefuls of no defined skill.

In many languages, the voyagers squeezed into their cabins had spoken of hope, of futures, of the blank sheet of new possibilities waiting for them. They had left behind the squalor of cities so old the very cockroaches were descended from those that had been crushed beneath the buckled feet of Goethe and Shakespeare: they had come with a few plates or bits of embroidered garments, leather-bound books with silverfish in the endpapers, or an engraving or two of Tower Bridge or the Danube, with a pair of candlesticks or their grandfather's chased silver double hunter, with their love of dumplings and pale ale, with their heads full of things in dark forests and wolves on cold plains, or of the way the Thames looked on a spring morning at Wapping: with all this useless baggage they had come, bursting with hope, to the Antipodes for a new life in a new land.

And what a land! Here, they had been told, the sun rose on the wrong side of the sky, stones lay upside down and the trees grew so thick together you could walk for miles along their crests. Now, on this glassy afternoon, their tiresome ship was passing between the headlands that were the gates to that new life, and all those weary folk were gesticulating at the foreign gum trees and asking their hearts what the future held.

My coming into existence was the main thing that made that day so special, but I am a person of magnanimous turn of mind, not one to hog the stage of history.

Up on deck those muddles of mixed people gaped at their first sight of their future, but down below in their cabin my thin woman and her brown-eyed man celebrated their new life in the way they loved to celebrate anything at all, or nothing in particular.

That balding man whispered in an oily language to that thin woman under him: *Darling,* he whispered, and caressed the bit of cheek beside her mouth, that favorite bit of his wife's face. *Darling, we have arrived,* he said, and for the last time they heard the mattress rustle and creak under them, and the pipes in the corner mocking them. It was an episode appropriate to such a significant moment: while my father groaned and my mother wept with the storms of pleasure he gave her, a vigorous questing tadpole was nosing into the skin of a ripe egg waiting to be courted, and in that moment's electric interchange, I, Joan, had my beginning.

Those two humans who had come together with lewd and effortful noises to conceive me, who were they, making history in a sound of sighs? Well, there was a thin woman, and a man chunky like a block of chopped wood, and balding so the dome of his cranium was egglike. The thin woman was thin by nature, not design, was in fact not in any way a woman of design, her long face, with its tanned-looking skin, having only its own features for adornment. She was a woman of narrow mobile lips with fine creases at their corners from years of finding things funny. When she smiled or laughed, gold glittered in that mouth, for back in the country they had left behind, that tiny country of werewolves and vampires, the father of the thin woman spent his days peering at molars, and loved nothing better than a bit of fine work on a gold inlay.

And the balding man, who was he? Just another stocky man in a lumpy cheap suit, with his father's signet ring on his little finger. He had always had a way of clutching at the handle of his heavy leather briefcase that had made the thin woman love him, there was such determination, and such innocent hope and purpose in that grip. In the briefcase, she had learned, was not much: a clean handkerchief, a notebook for great thoughts as they occurred, and a few bits of paper relating to enterprises that flickered and smouldered but never caught fire.

My love for you is hunger, he had whispered to the thin woman on the dentist's slippery couch, which during the day was the place where anxious folk squirmed and waited with their toothaches. *My love for you is hope. What is your thinking about a new life in a new land?* The thin woman loved this man in his suit that bulged and buckled, had loved him for a year or more, and had long ago decided that this was the man she wished to spend her life with. She was impatient with dentists and their cautions, their painstaking days fiddling with the endless decaying molars of folk stiff with the apprehension of pain, and was even willing to undergo the rigors of being foreign, and go to a new land on the bottom of the earth, to be with this man. He was a man of wit, a man given in a mild way to the extravagant gesture, and he was a man of intense brown eyes and a mouth that made most things plausible, but it was for none of this that the thin woman loved him. It was for his adoration of her that she loved him, knowing she would never again meet with a love like this.

My pink-scalped father panted, then, and groaned with the pain of adoring his wife, that no amount of penetrating her flesh could assuage, and while he panted and history was being made in the interior of a thin woman, other kinds of history were also being made.

In the new land they were approaching, men with frockcoats and small knowing eyes spoke of the birth of a nation, and thought with satisfaction of their fertile acres and the cash in their strongboxes. These were starchier folk, not eaters of garlic or wearers of rustic embroidery; they were folk who had never had to confront jellied eel, or the bailiff, on an empty stomach. They were folk made uneasy by gesticulation and suspicious of too much hope: they were men in frockcoats and side-whiskers that hid the shape of their faces, they were women with heavy cheeks made bland by privilege.

The birth of a nation, the men brayed, from their mouths concealed under heavy moustaches that smelled of mutton, and while they brayed and gestured, unknown to them cell merged with cell and I came into being. *Our debt to the mother country,* they intoned, and turned up their small eyes piously. They thought, or said they thought, that this was the moment at which this barbarous land was entering into its glory after a long and squalid beginning. It seemed important to them that this was the first year of the new century. Numbers mattered to these men, and it seemed glorious to them that this was the first year of the twentieth century: the number alone seemed rotund and full of promise, and they were sure they were making history. But the real history of that moment was known only to myself, where something as real as a human was being made.

JOAN MAKES HISTORY

SCENE ONE

In the year 1770 the continent that would become
known as Australia was claimed for Britain by
James Cook in the *Endeavour*. This is history, and
well known. Less well known is that I, Joan, was
there in one of my many manifestations, alongside
Cook.

MY husband the Captain, that famous man, has not had justice done to him in those portraits, and particularly not in those statues. He would never have stood in those grotesque postures, clutching a roll of bronze chart in front of his breeches in a somewhat suggestive way, as he is known to generations of sniggering children. He was a man of achievement, enough achievement to warrant moving his humble cottage stone by stone from the Old Country to the Antipodes. There are those who slyly hint that the cottage moved thus across the world was not the Captain's at all, but belonged to a pullet-breeding drunkard neighbor well known to him, and much disliked by him, and that the whole thing was a small joke at the expense of the colonials, but be that as it may. The Captain was a humble and agreeable man, his eyes mild and devoid of guile, and sharp enough to spot a man in a bush at fifty yards, although I knew, as most did not, that those fine eyes showed him only a world of variations on the color grey.

There were those who thought that I, as his wife, should be languishing patiently in the Old Country for him. But I was there with him on his voyage, for we were insep-

17

arable in spite of every risk, a couple so attached we would rather sink together than swim alone.

I had long loved my Captain, and had proved several times previously that my love was willing to undergo the rigors of ship life and harsh latitudes, and even to go to frightening far-off places to be near him. My father, a man of excessive deliberation, who measured out his words with the same care he took with the powders and poisons he kept in the forbidden jars in the dispensary: he had not hidden how much he doubted that lad of mine ever making good, no matter how many of his father's candles he squandered, hunching over books late into the night. But I had had faith, or perhaps I did not much care. Whether or not that lad of mine would ever make anything of himself, that lad was the one I wanted.

For me, the Captain was the only man on board, but there were others: numberless grimy sailors, naturally, and the slightly less grimy officers, Stubbs and Devereux and the rest, with their sextants and charts and small anxieties over matters of discipline and dignity. And then there were the scientific gentlemen, come to observe the goings-on at the bottom of the world, and put things in bottles, and press things between paper. There was the pasty pudgy Swede, who seemed always a little out of breath even when sitting down, there were the artists, whose job it was to draw things and make a record of the oddities we hoped to encounter, and then there was the man of leisure, the dandy, the philanderer: the botanical gentleman.

On the day the ship sailed for parts unknown, he had come aboard lightly springing up the ladder. He had landed in front of me, pink in the cheeks, and stood before me with a pleased smile already in place. He was a small smooth man with a tight smile of some charm and tiny white teeth, and I could see that he thought himself irresistible to any creature in a skirt, and never missed the chance to charm whatever kind of female was at hand, in case she proved susceptible to later seduction.

I could see that the Captain felt no great love for this hummingbird of a man, with his quick eyes and brilliant waistcoat of silver brocade that shimmered in the sun, when good honest broadcloth, and a smile that was as rare as gold, were good enough for my plain Captain.

When the botanist was presented to me he held my hand in both of his—and what small soft hands his were, so that my own felt ragged and gigantic—and bent over it murmuring for much longer than was necessary to pay his respects. I caught enough of his low tones to know that he thought it worth his while to flatter me, and when his hyperbole came to an end he gazed at me in a way that a more foolish woman might have allowed to make her heart flutter. But I, as well as being a woman of considerable Yorkshire shrewdness, was a woman of great plainness of feature. I knew that no dandy in brocade would ever languish after me, and certainly not at first sight, as the sighing botanist was pretending to, so I turned away from his posturing and watched as England slid away behind us.

The mystery of our voyage, the end we all wondered about, was the Great South Land, one last bit of the globe on which, if it existed, no flag had yet been raised to claim ownership. They tried to conceive of their Great South Land, all those men in the great cabin of the ship, serious in their jackets and braid. They showed me their spidery maps, tracing with their forefingers the ghostly fringe of something that the Dutch and others had stumbled on and not wanted. *They reported it the barrenest land they had ever seen,* Stubbs of the long face reminded us. *They did not want it, why should His Majesty?* Stubbs of the lugubrious dewlaps, a good man with an astrolabe

19

but no smiler, imagined this land as a long thin piece of sand and rock, providing nothing more rewarding than cliffs for foolhardy Dutchmen to smash themselves upon.

The Captain was more sanguine, and stood spinning his globe for me, demonstrating how the world was unbalanced for lack of a continent in the Southern Ocean. He dealt with the world gently: it was not only that the globe swinging so silkily under his palm was not his own property, but was that of His Majesty's Government: it was that the Captain handled the world with reverence, and his palm shaped itself around its comfortable curves as if warming it, coaxing it to bring forth its secrets and deliver to him the long-awaited Great South Land.

It may be nothing much, I warned him, not wanting him to suffer too great a disappointment. *It may be a scattering of islands, nothing more, or a land of desert and stones.* The Captain was a mild man, and not prone to saying *no:* rather he nodded in a vague sort of way, and said *That is possible* in a considering manner, so no one's feelings could be injured: but I knew that he was not discouraged, and that he hoped for great things from his Great South Land.

That land lay somewhere ahead of us, if it lay at all, steaming and swelling, growing humid and huge in our imaginings with its jungles and waterfalls, its waiting nuggets and tigers. Towards that patient land our tiny vessel bounced and leaped, rocked and surged through the ocean swells, straining at every bit of rope and every creaking block and tackle, bristling with beings.

I clung to a shroud, peering westward, for I was sick of sea breezes and strange ports now, and impatient to see that Great South Land. It was proving more elusive than anything so great should have been, so that we folk on the upper deck were coming to know each other rather better than we wished.

Oh, that botanical gentleman! He became tiresome, finding me alone in sheltered corners of the deck, standing there blocking my sun while he flattered and invented and gave me many fine glances from under his immaculate eyebrows. *Ah,* he would sigh, *Ah my dear, if you only knew how I lie awake during these long nights!* The look he gave me was intended to cause my pulse to race and my head to fill with inflamed imaginings. But the simpering botanist buttered no parsnips with me. I knew my sturdy Yorkshire face gave him no encouragement, and did not bother to conceal that he was nothing more to me than an insect buzzing at my ear or a pup whining around my ankles.

I had not always been a woman so impervious to blandishment. It was all the easier to resist the botanist because on another occasion I had failed to resist a man of the same lying and wheedling nature. I had betrayed the Captain once, and been forgiven, and I had seen with fear how close I had been to losing him.

So the botanist got short shrift from me: such a fop was repugnant, but even if he had not been, I would have continued to spurn his advances. I gave him nothing: not a look, not a smile, not a single touch of flesh, only the back of my hard hand, when on some pretext he would seize it and press his lips on it. He got nothing from me, and I saw how the sluggish Swede watched, and provoked the botanist to further excesses with disparaging remarks on his entire lack of success.

Then the dandy turned. Being a coward as well as a dandy, he did not attack the woman who was spurning him, but her husband. Nothing this botanist could say, no amount of poetry panted out to me in the lee of the wheelhouse, could diminish my husband in my eyes: but this man, cunning as one of the reptiles he pickled for posterity, knew that there was another way to punish the Captain for the fidelity of his wife.

This Great South Land of yours, he said, and allowed his lip to curl. *My dear captain, I admire your earnestness of purpose in sailing to the end of the world for it, but between you and me, I had it from my cousin at the Admiralty that the whole thing is a small jest at your expense that had the rear-admiral amused for a morning or two.* There was no escaping him as we all sat glumly chewing through salt pork and pease. There were nights, in the glare of the swinging lantern, when I longed for a tempest of the kind that would send our plates tipping to the floor, and make our scientific gentleman go green as waves crashed over the poop.

But the Captain was not a man to be shaken by the gibes of any flighty gentleman in a brocade waistcoat, and he and I had laughed in private at the way the botanist was courting me. *Just the same, sir,* he said in his calm way, that made people become very still, listening hard in case they missed the words: *Just the same, those are my instructions, and I intend to carry them out.* The botanist pushed at a bit of pork on his plate and smiled, a smile too engaging to be quite true, a smile of too many white teeth between which the tip of his tongue was suggestively pink. *But my dear captain,* he crowed, like a nasty tropical bird with his teeth and flashing waistcoat, *My dear sir, you cannot really expect to find this phantom of a Great South Land!* He went on staring at the Captain, who was taking refuge now in being punctilious about cutting a morsel of fat off his pork, and finally the botanist let out a laugh that was a cry of contempt, and exclaimed: *Is is possible that you are simple enough to believe you will find it?* The shrill spurned dandy was becoming hysterical in his inability to excite his phlegmatic Captain, and a line of inelegant spittle

22

was forming in one corner of that mouth of his, a mouth that never stopped smiling, although the muscles on either side of it were visibly straining in the effort to remain amused and scornful. The Captain munched on without responding, and only a wife who had watched him toiling by candlelight to reach a position that this popinjay had attained by birth could have observed the way his large hands, which had come late to the finicky business of refined manners at table, strangled his knife and fork.

Each dawn lit up the banal horizon to the west and showed it as innocent as ever of any land, let alone a Great South Land. The Captain, never a man of many words, became more and more silent, and in the short warm nights he held me tightly against him and squeezed my hand in his large capable one, but was silent except for his sighs. When his eyes opened in the mornings, the Great South Land was his first thought: his second was that slimy triumphant botanist, sleeker as each day passed with nothing on the horizon. I lay watching the captain of my life, and saw the way his eyes flew open on hope with each dawn, and the way he strode to the porthole in his nightshirt, straining out at the smug smooth sea.

The Captain is amusingly earnest, I find, I overheard the botanist drawling to the lard-faced Swede, and laughing: then, the hypocrite, he pretended to realize of a sudden that I was behind him, and removed the laugh from his face. He bowed his vile small bow, and exclaimed in his most unctuous and fluid way, *Why bless my soul! I was only saying to the good doctor here how much we do admire your husband's persistence and what a great disappointment and what a shame for him it is indeed.*

I could not answer, though many words rose to my lips, some from surprising pithy Yorkshire recesses of my memory. I turned away from the wink I caught between him and the Swede, a wink I was intended to catch, and intended to be injured by, and had taken a step away from him when suddenly he seized my wrist hard and with his other hand tweaked painfully at my cheek in the way uncles do to little girls. I pulled away, but he kept his savage grip on my wrist, so I could feel some ring or other pressing deeply into my flesh, and he tweaked and tweaked at my cheek. In spite of all the Captain had warned me of, in the way of keeping things civil and if possible staying on his good side, I had drawn breath to shriek at the way he was assaulting me when he let me go and cried out *There! It is off! They leave a most terribly disfiguring sting, my dear lady, which would have altogether marred your loveliness.* Now he stood back and showed his teeth at me, while I stood flushed and furious.

But at last the day came when the doubters were forced to swallow their sneers. *Land ho,* the cry came down from the crow's nest, and everyone peered up into the bright sky at the speck of man flapping his hat towards the west. The Captain was not a man to become agitated in front of his minions, but I, who knew him better than anyone, saw how his hands were gripping the rail so hard the skin had gone pale. I saw he had to tell himself to remain upright and not strain forward over the rail like someone at a bear pit, in his eagerness to see his dream become the reality of a low dark line on the horizon. He turned to Devereux and said in the most leisurely way, as if it did not matter in the least, *My telescope, if you please, Mr Devereux.* Devereux handed it to him and I saw how he paused before he lifted it to his eye, to make sure his hands would not shake and give anyone the chance to snigger. The botanist with his brocade and small sneering mouth was mercifully below, fiddling with flora in his cabin, and I was happy that this great moment for the Captain was unspoiled by that smooth contemptuous man.

He lifted the brass telescope to his eye, squinting at glare. He had always been a man who had loved to spy out the unseen and to guess at the half-known, and had always loved that telescope. Now he gazed through it while I imagined what it might be showing him; voids of sky, distant dark vegetation, perhaps thin blue smoke from fires lit by people as yet unknown. When at last he lowered the telescope, full of what he had seen, I thanked the Lord who had watched over us that the botanist was still below, for it seemed that Jack the cabin boy had failed to polish the brass properly, and the Captain stood with a black eye where he had pressed it against the eyepiece. I had to look away, and I saw Devereux, who was a good man, and Stubbs, who was a fool but knew better than to laugh at his captain, look away too, so none of us would be forced into a guffaw at the way the Captain stood solemn like a badger with a black eye.

My dour Captain smiled seldom, but when he looked around at Stubbs and Devereux, and at me, he was smiling in a way to dim the sun, his face creasing into those unaccustomed lines. *Make a note, Mr Devereux, for the log,* he said calmly, but his eyes were on me, and the words were made jubilant by that smile. *Make a note: at a quarter of three in the afternoon, the Great South Land was sighted.*

JOAN

THERE were those who doubted my existence, women slack with childbearing who assured the thin woman that the rigors of the voyage were enough to explain the gap she was noticing in the cycles of her months, those who assured her that in this upside-down land such signs did not always mean anything. *Perhaps,* she told the bald man. *Or perhaps not.* There seemed a sort of hush over them, in spite of the clamor and anxieties of settling in the new land, of buying pots and pans and learning what to do with mutton, and having halting conversations in the new language with people who shouted at them.

But when the thin woman began to be sick, pale and peaky in the mornings, craving food and sickened by it at once, when she began to quaff jug after jug of water and still thirst, when she began to sleep longer and longer, and still need sleep: these paradoxes began to inform them that I was there. At last the thin woman became no longer thin, and when she could no longer make her buttons meet because I was lengthening within her, she and the balding man doubted no longer.

Would his creature be a female, the balding man speculated: a dazzling beauty with teasing copper curls and a smile that would make rocks crumble where they stood?

His heart clenched with the foreshadowed pain of seeing his untouchable exquisite daughter become a woman, of seeing her eyes grow red, languishing after some unworthy oaf, of sitting up late at night, waiting for her to be returned to him from some night of dancing, or worse, and of seeing in her swollen lips that she was no longer his pure girl, but was a woman, defiled by the lust of some man. That was pain: that she would no longer belong to her father, but to the world, to strangers who would not care as he did, for he would lay down his life a thousand times for her: strangers who would make her bored, make her weep, perhaps even raise a cad's hand against her and bruise her white skin. Were there worse pains? Yes, that of having not a peach-skinned copper-curled girl, but an angular hairy-faced lank dolt of a girl with no more sparkle or loveliness than a cold sausage.

If it was a boy! The bald man's mind leapt to two images: one of the limp body of his son, killed in a duel at dawn, a ridiculous fear but his picture of dread: the other of his son in a dark suit, unrecognizable to his father because of the grave look on his face, accepting the keys or crown of government, and himself bursting into tears from sheer fullness of proud heart.

Well, all this I guessed, and some I heard, as the bald man mused aloud to the thin woman, who smiled and nodded as she counted the stitches on the tiny garment she was knitting. I heard secrets, too, from my tight red hiding place. I heard that guttural man, who loved his wife like an addiction, groaning over her body and laughing at the way she swelled with me. He laid his hand over the curves of her belly, warming me inside, feeling my life stirring there: I could feel his hand reverent on the thin woman's skin, and tremulous with the possibilities he felt within. I felt him lowering his large head towards me, ear first, and sensed how he became congested, holding his breath, trying to listen to the quick flicker of my heartbeat. *My darling,* he whispered, *you are most precious, even when grotesque.* I felt the thin woman—not so thin now—shake with laughter and I laughed too, as she was doing, fondly, at this man who watched her with eyes soft with adoration.

I swelled and caused the thin woman to swell, I laughed and cavorted in my warm room, for my job was simple: to wait and to grow. When I began to kick and jab at the thin woman with my elbow, they remembered that I was waiting to join them, and made ready. As well as the tiny knitted garments, and the others laboriously stitched and smocked, the thin woman obtained a cradle, and they both crowed and exclaimed over it, and planned how I would look, lying in it perfect and peachlike.

In the end I was impatient at the limitations of my space: my legs kicked out, longing to stretch, and I arched and thrashed against the muscle and bone that held me. Yet when they began to release me, I fought against the tide that was forcing me down and out. *Self!* I cried. *Thin woman! How can you turn against me like this?* Oh, I wept in my wetness, and struggled, and clawed at the slippery walls of my nest, but there was no resisting those muscles squeezing against me, no turning back from destiny now.

It was the greatest moment of my history, without which there would be no further moments, although to the hard-handed doctor and the Sister in her starch, I was nothing more great than yet another baby, wrinkled like a prune and as anonymous as a ham. Even the mother, lying back triumphant at last, and the bald father tremulous later with his bunch of flowers, did not relish the greatness of this moment. They turned away from me lying puckered in pink, and the man who had contributed his tadpole to the making of me took the hand

31

of the woman who had done the rest: pale now, sunken into her pillows, full-eyed with our struggle. *My precious one,* he whispered, *I thought I would lose you for ever.* His voice shook with feeling, for he loved this thin woman of his, whom I had nearly done to death in our battle. His voice shook, his soft eyes filled with tears, and his hands warmed the bloodless dulled hands of his wife as if to infuse her with his own strength. She could not speak, the woman whose hand was being crushed, but did not mind the pain of her husband's love around her hand, now the other pain was over, and she managed some sort of a smile that revealed the gold tooth teasing at the side of her mouth and showed him that, balding, egglike, trembling, fearful, uncertain though he was at this moment, she would never feel anything for him but the tenderest love.

There they were then, making their pacts of skin and soft looks together, and I lay unwrinkling like a beetle. I was preparing for great things, though they, myopic of vision, tiny of mind, feeble in their grasp of the largeness of life, knew none of it: they had no inkling that history lay in the room with them, quietly sucking at the air of the brand-new world.

JOAN MAKES HISTORY

SCENE TWO

In 1788 a fleet of ships landed at Botany Bay with the purpose of establishing a British colony there. On board were convicts male and female, and marines, and of course myself, Joan.

I was snivelling, lecherous, a despiser of men and a woman with a skilled shrill way with a useful lie. For having been caught bold as brass relieving a gentleman of his gold fob-watch in broad daylight, I had been sentenced to be transported to the bottom of the earth for the term of my natural life, considered expendable by the authorities of my native land, but I was not one to be cowed by the chilly schemes of His Majesty's Government. I had decided that, of all the feet on this unhappy fleet of ships, mine would be the first to soil the new land.

As prisoners of His Majesty, we were not allowed up on deck at this historic moment, the landing at Botany Bay, but we heard the thunder of the anchor chain through water and felt the slimy boards shake under us. It was a sound we had not heard for many weeks, or it could have been months or years, for none of us had cared enough in the beginning to keep track of the days, and now the uncounted flow of time swept us along like animals. I was locked in among weak, puling women who had moaned and cried, cowered and shivered and ineffectually rubbed at their arms all the way from the Thames, rubbing at gooseflesh even in the smelly tropics.

35

Their crimes were as timid as they were themselves: they had filched a handkerchief, or threepence worth of cheese, or slept on the wrong doorstep and been discovered: even in crime they were gormless, and now I was sick to death of them. *Give me a man!* I had shrieked often enough on our voyage, and one-eyed Betsy had cackled in her hoarse way, *Give him to me after, love, I have never minded the second suck at a bottle,* but at this moment I had greater things to think of than men and their pathetic bottles of lust.

It was like stripping skin, paring flesh from flesh, to peel off boots, stockings, skirts, petticoats, bodice, until I stood in the hold, my skin green in that light, with a ring of silent sick women around me, staring as though they had never before seen a nipple, or flesh in quantity. *I will now make history,* I said loudly, so the women blinked at me in a considering way. But I knew these women, and I knew that nothing like consideration was going on behind their blinking eyes: nothing more interesting than the blossoming thought that my boots, sad creatures though they were, and my skirts stiff with the filth of a year, might be better than their own and might, now they were stripped from the flesh of their owner, become available to one of these blinking women who was short of a boot or two. *I will make history, and the devil take all those men and their red coats and strutting,* I cried and, breasts swinging loose so the women blinked more, went to the hatch high on the side of the ship, where in fine weather we could take in turns the pleasure of a faceful of fresh air and the kiss of spray on our dirty cheeks.

It was too high for me to climb through, but I was about to make history and would not be held back by any such feeble physical obstacle as a bit of height. *Dot,* I shouted into Dot's unblinking face, which was aghast at my flesh shaking before her in all its majesty, *You can make history too, Dot, give me a leg up.* Dot had never heard of history, you could tell by the way she looked scared and opened her mouth as if to understand this difficulty by eating it. But even Dot, big feeble Dot, knew what a leg up was, and was frightened enough by the way I was shouting and gesturing at her to make her hands a calloused cradle, and be my clumsy midwife into the new world.

You will go and drown, Agnes said in her lugubrious way. *You will drown, Joan, when you hit that water, or be swallowed by something, some eel.* But eels did not frighten me as much as the prospect of an adventure caused the blood to pulse in my veins. *Damn the eels,* I cried, *and Agnes, I was a mudlark when you were slime in your mother's belly and I can swim like a fish, watch if you dare!*

All the same, when Dot's hard hands propelled me up and out through the hatch and there was nothing but air, sun, blinding water, and the alarming sound of nothing but space, for a moment I was jammed by my hips in the hatch, which had not been made with the egress of large-hipped women in mind, and I was afraid. I felt them pushing and thrusting at my feet: now it felt as if they were eager to push me out, conspiring to expel me, and all at once I was not so sure I wanted to be expelled: that vile hold seemed like home and was for a moment preferable to the bright unknown beyond.

I hit the water shrieking, for in the end I burst out of that hatch like a cork out of old beer, head first and flailing into water that was a shock like a shout on my skin. The water was an explosion of blue, of wet, of clean, so that I screamed as it took me in and I felt the silver bubbles caress my cheeks. There was terror, too, in being weightless, unbound, in nothing but space, for

the first time in so many months. The great cry that only
the blue water heard was the cry of a being in bliss and
fear, bursting into some new world or other.

When I came up and breathed air again the ship was
black and sullen, sitting on the water full of the vomit
and anguish of months. On the deck a man or two pointed
at me, and there below them at the hatch were the pale
moon faces of the women. I could hear feeble piping
shouts, and a shrill cry from one of the women at the
hatch, that had an encouraging sound, although birdlike
and unclear to my water-filled ears.

I turned away from that dark and wormy hulk sitting
on the water, and struck out boldly, my breath coming
short and painful with the excitement, and with the
exercise I was unused to, so that I began to splutter and
take some of this large blue bay into my gullet, and had
to float for a moment on my back, fighting the panic of
liberty. I reminded myself of my destiny, which was to
be the first foreign foot to touch the rim of this land,
and floundered on, toward a bit of yellow sand between
the trees. I was wheezing, sinking, almost ready to despair
of my destiny, when I saw that the water was becoming
shallow and pale, and I forced myself on with reminders
of how glorious it would be to cheat the Captain of his
triumph, until at last there was sand underfoot, and I
stepped with my unsavory feet onto the Great South
Land.

We had the continent to ourselves for a short while:
briefly it was just myself and the people who lived there,
whom I glimpsed from the corner of my eye, but who
were never where I was looking. But it was not long
before the pinnace approached from the ship, and I
prepared to surrender my moment of freedom.

I watched as the sailors lifted the Captain and his
officers from the boat and carried them the last few yards

through the wash to the beach: the ceremonial braid-piped tailcoats of these important men would run blue down all the white breeches if they became wet, and the dignity of the occasion would be sadly marred. Later I watched from between two redcoats who held me more tightly than was necessary as everyone tried to make a bit of drama out of it all: soldiers fired a salute, the flagpole was finally persuaded to stay upright in the thin stony soil, the chaplain stumbled through the words in his book: *In the name of His Majesty,* and the prayer was droned through to its loud *Amen.*

All this you will read in any book, but what you will not read there are the sordid secrets of that moment. You will not read that mine was the first foot ashore, or that a white woman (or at least a grey one), her nakedness insufficiently hidden beneath a piece of canvas sailcloth, was present when that wrinkled flag was raised. Nor will you read of how the ceremonial jackets of all those important men, unfolded after months in a sea chest, stank of damp and mildew and the stale old sweat of other splendid moments. When the flag had been raised, no time was lost in tearing off those foul jackets and flinging them over bushes in the hope that the glaring sun might cauterize the smell.

With the flag planted, already listing in its hole—or did everything look crooked after all those months at sea?—it was hard to know what to do next. The fact had been announced: this piece of nasty land (which was already proving itself rich in small persistent insects if in nothing else), was now a part of Britain, a blank new land waiting to have its history written on it. The silent dark people watching from their secret places knew this to be a lie, but the invaders did not.

Anyone could see that this was a great moment of history, but above the flagpole a crowd of birds was

39

becoming hysterical in a tree, laughing like lunatics through long beaks. I fancied the idea of a land where the ground repelled flagpoles stuck in it, and where the birds did no feeble tweeting, but gave forth mockery. *This is a land after my own heart,* I decided, and I joined the birds. Mine was not only the first foreign foot to step ashore: mine was also the first foreign laugh to sound out, sharp and rude, across the waters of Botany Bay.

JOAN

THERE were no real uncles in my childhood, to ask me what I was going to be when I grew up, and give me threepenny pieces. But there was Uncle Laszlo from the flat downstairs, and there were his many sisters, who spent long hours with my mother in the kitchen producing slippery food in crockery pots. Uncle Laszlo was fond of asking me what I was going to be, never tiring of my answer and never failing in his response. *I will make history,* I told Uncle Laszlo each time, and each time he and Father would laugh and slap their thighs, and exclaim *Good luck on you, then, Joan,* trying to sound like the men they heard on the streets. Then the many sisters of Laszlo would come from the kitchen to find out what so much mirth and thigh-slapping was all about, and the whole thing would be translated for them so they could all laugh too, and exclaim in foreign syllables, and remind themselves they had come to a country nude of any history to speak of, so little Joan had the right idea, planning to make some.

No history is to be made in the dull wastes of childhood. I spent mine set apart from all the others in the playground, being ashamed of the thick dark bread made by my mother, of which my sandwiches were constructed, and the olives in my lunch-box, and the reek of garlic from our kitchen. I was embarrassed too, by the way my skin was always brown, even in winter: all the other girls were pale puddings of people who made sure sunlight never darkened their skins, and they would not have wanted to be me.

Even more than all this, I was shamed by my foreign gold-toothed mother, with her smiling helpless inability to make herself understood, so that I had to stand twisting one foot behind the other, mulishly translating for her at the butcher's and the greengrocer's, and having those large red-fisted men shouting at me as if I, too, was stupid and foreign.

My poor bemused mother was baffled by most things in this country, where the birds frightened her with their mirth, and the sun threatened to fry her where she stood. The shapeless folk of this land did not bother to conceal that they thought she must be an imbecile not to be able to say *Fine weather for ducks* when they said *Wet enough for you?* as they wrapped a parcel of best neck on the marble counter, while the savage antipodean rain poured down outside the shop. She was baffled, and did not ask her stranger-daughter much, because her daughter was impatient at her own clumsiness with the language they shared. She had not grown into a slant-eyed, catlike smooth young girl, such as the mother had been back in the suave old country, but was becoming a tall, loud, bold-eyed girl who laughed too loudly and too knowingly.

Even my father, although able at least to exchange an approximation of those phrases with the other fathers, held his cigarette in a way none of them did, and could not be relied on to react in the proper way to small remarks on the weather or the price of wool (being likely, to my humiliation, to embark on a long guttural speech about the climates of nations and the price of freedom):

44

even he could not make me feel anything but an alien.
How lucky they were, Phyllis and Gladys and all the
rest, whose fathers knew how to get the fire going at a
picnic, and could deal with a puncture on their bikes
without, as my father did, becoming flushed and manic,
turning the nuts the wrong way!

Those lucky girls went home to solid houses with front
lawns, not muddled buildings cut up into many small
flats. There they did their homework at one end of the
worn table in the kitchen, licking the tips of their pencils
until their tongues were purple, laboring over arithmetic
and parsing. At the other end of the table their mother
peeled potatoes comfortably, and out on the verandah
their father sat in his singlet with a long glass of beer
perspiring in his hand. Those fathers were made uneasy
by all the foreign philosophizing of my father, and despised such incompetence with fires and nuts, and were
wary of so much accent, that meant you could never be
a hundred percent sure the bloke was not having a bit
of a go at you, with his long words. So they mocked me,
all those classmates, taunting me in the playground for
the way my father was bald as well as foreign, and the
way my mother looked funny with a scarf on her head.
Was she bald as well, they wanted to know?

When we arrived at a certain age, all those tidy girls
with their neat fish-paste sandwiches put out large ma-
tronly busts under their tunics. I, still as flat of chest as
a wall, watched and hankered after them with hankies
down my own front. I loved their melting flesh when I
saw them changing after our feeble games with bat and
ball. I could barely resist running a palm over those rolls
of biscuit-colored flesh above their petticoat elastic, and
I longed to touch the gleaming shoulders under the straps
that cut into them.

They were shy, though, these flawless women, and their mouths became prim as they dressed in the chilly change room. They turned away from me and put their elbows up like bats to do up their blouses at the back, or writhed under their robes, becoming red in the face, and did not emerge from underneath until they were fully dressed, so I missed the moistness of thighs where suspenders snapped against soft hairless flesh, and the shadows between breast and underarm.

I joked and cavorted, clowning at my own expense, because to make them laugh would have been a kind of acceptance, but their faces never showed much besides distaste. I even learned rounders to win their approval, and enjoyed the galloping, and the yelling, and although I found the game absurd, this dotty parody of the boys at cricket, there was a pleasure in belting away at the ball, and in seeing those smug faces distort and go crooked when, by accident of course, I struck their smooth shins with my bat. In my desire to please, and in a sort of rage of contempt, I even ran fiercely around the oval, pretending I cared enough about their absurd game to want to train for it, like some silly seal.

When that failed too, I tried to make a good story out of it all. *My grandmother was a vampire,* I told them. *She was from Transylvania, where all the vampires come from.* This was the truth, for my long-dead grandmother really had lived in Transylvania, although on the tinted picture we had of the place, it seemed to be grass and sky like anywhere else. Because it was the truth, I had to try to make it more interesting, so I looked shifty, askance, as if I was inventing this tale which was in fact the truth. The girls became confused then, and fell to thinking with satisfaction about their own grandmothers from Dural or Woy Woy, who knitted matinee jackets and bootees, and had nothing foreign or peculiar about them.

As my youth progressed, Uncle Laszlo and Father spent longer and longer talking gravely in the old language, and there seemed more and more for them to be grave about. Out on the streets, Mother began to be the victim of scowls and things muttered behind hands. In the playground the girls explained with satisfaction that they could not speak to me any more because I was a *filthy Hun*, and Australians were at war with *filthy Huns*. The more I tried to explain, with my feeble grasp of geography, that being from Translyvania was not the same as being a *filthy Hun*, the more their faces closed against me.

Mother wept one night: Father had come home pale, his baldness leaving his face exposed under the blast of emotion, and spread out a piece of paper on the table where the light rained down on it. With a finger under the words, he read, so loudly it made my ears hurt: *To Whom All Persons Shall Come*. I could see Mother was already lost, but Father's moving finger moved on: *Am desirous of abandoning and renouncing the use of the name Victor Radulescu*. His finger shook, as his voice did, as he caressed the sounds of his own name: *I hereby absolutely renounce and abandon the said name of Victor Radulescu*.

Then, paler than ever, with the points of his cheekbones making the skin of face tight, he used his thick-nibbed fountain-pen to cross out *Joan Radulescu* in all my books and replace it with *Joan Redman*. Finally he brought out the *Atlas of Australia* over which he pored from time to time, memorizing Australian towns and rivers. *Here, Joan*, he said. *We are loyal Australians, and must put the map right*. From his briefcase he took out a newspaper and peered at it, then at the map of South Australia, scratching and rewriting: *Hahndorf* into *Ambleside, Blumberg* into

Birdwood, Rosenthal into *Rosedale.* When he had finished, the color had returned to his face. *There, Joan. No one can accuse us now.*

Those Abercrombies and Smiths were not fooled, though, by Miss Gibbs crossing out *Joan Radulescu* in the roll book and inking in *Joan Redman. It is not your real name,* they pointed out at wearisome length in the playground. *It can never really be your real name.*

As we all grew older, and the others grew more and more womanly of form, they gathered in clusters and whispered about their boys and their prospects and their possessions. They all wanted the same kinds of prospects and possessions, and even wanted the same boy, the son of a doctor, who was a particularly good prospect. I had seen this boy, who seemed to me no kind of prospect at all, but a lad overextended and puny of limb, like a potato sprouting in the dark.

They clustered and giggled, those silly girls, and pretended to each other that their stockings and frocks mattered to them for their own sakes, and that the hours they spent with mirrors, trying their hair parting on the other side, or a pair of combs or a daring red ribbon, were for themselves alone. They could not admit that they were biding their time and preparing themselves for their dream. But what a secondhand dream theirs was! It was to marry a prospect, to be the colorless wife of an ambition, to wash the socks and underpants of a destiny.

None of them would ever burst into any flame more dramatic than their one day in white. Even then, their faces would be cross with anxiety until afterwards, when the confetti would catch their eyelids and they would kindle for a few moments, so the photographs would catch them laughing into the teeth of their grooms. But they would not blaze later that night in the honeymoon

suite at the Royal with their large-knuckled boy: he might
have had prospects, but he would have no more idea of
a good time in passion than would a silly dog humping
on your leg.

Such were my scathing thoughts on the subject of these
women I could never resemble, and whom I envied while
I despised. I knew things would always be different for
me: I knew I wished not to marry history, but to make
it.

I took consolation in planning many histories for myself, each one larger than the last. *I will be a great writer,*
I told myself, staring at a cloud in a soulful sort of way.
Or I will be Prime Minister, and I thought with pleasure
of how the girls would not sniff in that dismissive way
then, but admire me at last. Unlike these feeble creatures
I was forced to spend my days with, I was not blind to
the beckoning finger of history, or deaf to the clarion
calls of destiny. I wished to make the earth shiver on its
axis with some large action or other, whose precise shape
would be revealed to me in due course.

JOAN MAKES HISTORY

SCENE THREE

By 1795 the colony was established and George
Bass, Matthew Flinders, and a cabin boy set off to
map the coastline, but a storm forced them ashore
at Providence Bay, and there they encountered a
group of Aboriginal inhabitants. I, Joan, was one
of the people they found.

I longed to make my mark. How to make it I did not know, but I tried: something in me drove me on to make something that had not been made before, and leave something to show where I had been. I made my mark in secret on the roofs of the caves that had not been singled out by the men as theirs: I would slip away from the shrill women with their digging sticks and daub with ochre, rubbing and smearing, trying to say something on a bit of flat rock.

Those silly women! They knew that I was set apart from them: they knew out of the corners of their eyes when I went, and when I returned, and the children spied on me, so there was no concealing what I was doing. What tomfoolery, what a silly waste of time it seemed to them, when there were roots to dig, and seeds to grind, and hilarity to share under a tree!

The women did not envy me or admire me for wanting to mess about with bits of colored mud, but thought that I was to be pitied for my unexpected ideas. Warra was the destiny that others thought was awaiting me: Warra by my side, his children coming out of my body, my hands wrapping his bones in bark at the end. I knew Warra too well already: my betrothed was a dull young

53

man who listened hard to the uncles and was a fine person. Stolid Warra, who never lost patience with the children when they became tiresome about things! Amiable Warra, never less than intelligently deferential, even to old Kulurra, who had a tendency to dribble and dodder by afternoon: good, kind Warra, for whom I was envied by those mild gigglers with their blameless hearts! Warra would be my man, would be joined flesh of my flesh when I was of age, Warra's hands would finger my skin in the nights, Warra would exclaim as he shot and pulsed into me.

But although he was such a worthy and had eyes for no one but me, Warra was not a person who made me laugh. Although no one else doubted my future, I did: a restlessness, the same itch that drove me to dab with ochre in caves, told me that I must have a larger destiny than Warra, digging sticks, and children. Somewhere another destiny waited its moment.

So I waited for life to blossom, and at last it did. A vessel careened into the thunderous beach by the lagoon, a long vessel that threatened to tip at every swell of the sea behind it, and spill the three strangers out into the cold Wattamolla water. The vessel came to rest at last in the shallows where the lagoon ran into the surf, and I saw that my chance had come.

There were three strangers: a tall one, a short puny one, and a boy in the back of the boat, so young as to be beardless. But it was the tall one I watched: he was the first ashore, plainly the leader. He was bulky in the coverings that clung to his body and thick in the legs and trunk. His skin was a nasty clay color, and his hair was as straight as grass, and hung down over his forehead in a way that made him look low of brow. He was a dreadful man to look at, and he set the other girls giggling behind their hands so their breasts shook, and even the

older women stared and tittered as he tried to stride from
his boat, and stumbled on a wave so he nearly fell. He
was a tall man, but a little weak of ankle, it could be
seen, and perhaps that unnatural hair weakened him, for
he tottered for a moment in the wash as if his balance
was gone.

Here was a man from an unknown world, where living
men looked the color of the dead, a man to be pitied
for his shabby skin and his clumsiness with a wave.

The uncles walked slowly down the beach towards the
strangers, but to my indignation the women chivvied us
girls up the beach towards the lagoon, where we could
see nothing, and hear only the muted roar and hiss of
the waves.

The girls snickered and screeched and became shrill
and birdlike on the subject of what the tall one was hiding
under his coverings. Would it be pale like a witchetty
grub, drooping out of a nest of lifeless strands like those
on his head? Or was it all different under the coverings,
as brown as any other man's? They became incoherent,
trying to imagine how it would be to have such a man
lie on top of you and somehow extract his grub from its
coverings, how it might be to see that earthy flesh close
up, and what kind of slippery strangeness that lank hair
might be.

I did not titter, but sat hugging my knees and trying
to shut out the silliness of the girls so I could plan
something magnificent, and at last we all became tired
of the lagoon and the gigglers ran out of lewd imaginings.
Finally the older women levered themselves up off the
grass one by one and wandered as if absentmindedly back
down towards the beach. We followed quietly, in case
the women remembered and sent us back again away
from the fun.

If I had not been different, a cut above those other flighty girls, I too would have squealed and pointed and rocked all over again with laughing at what we saw on the beach. The tall stranger had a shiny thing in his hands that glittered in the sun, and had reassured our cautious menfolk of his friendly intentions by cutting their beards and hair. The men sat gravely along the dune waiting their turn, and were becoming huge of eye, seeing their familiar friends transforming before their eyes into bald strangers.

The tall man did not look around, not for the longest time, although his small companion and the boy with his pale mouth ajar could not seem to stop staring at us girls. The small one spoke in a voice strangled by something, as if a skein of lust was tangled in his throat, and he could not keep his eyes off our breasts in the sun, for all the world as if he had never before seen a breast in sunlight. He spoke, and the lad opened his mouth wider in a laugh that showed brown and broken teeth, and that made the tall one straighten up from snipping the curls of an uncle. When the tall one replied to the short one, he was abashed, and even the lad closed his mouth on his bad teeth. The sun seemed to fade for a moment as solemnity hung over all of us. The tall one bent again to the uncle on his dune, but there were few curls left to snip on that head now, and it was time for the next.

Who was the next man sitting along the dune fingering the hair on his head? It was none other than Warra my betrothed, standing to receive the silver thing on his hair, standing nearly as tall as the stranger, though not as wide. Knowing him as I did, I saw that Warra was afraid, although so many brave uncles had survived the cutting, and he hid his fear behind a scowl that took the smile from the face of the stranger, who glanced around as if

uncertain, wobbling again on his weak ankles in the face
of such a frown.

Then it was that I made history, bounding down from
my dune, sand spurting between my toes, until I stood
before him, and held out my own curls. He watched as
if unsure what I meant, but I knew he was not stupid,
but merely being cautious. At last he did what I wanted:
I stood so close I could snuff up nosefuls of his musty
smell, and he snipped the curls from my head one by
one.

He stood over me snipping until there was little left
to snip, while the uncles watched gravely as if waiting
for me to turn into a reptile—a goanna perhaps—or
sprout a penis from my ear, and Warra's frown wore
itself so deeply into his face it seemed like a crease in a
rockfold. He shifted from foot to unhappy foot until the
sand was weary: I knew he itched to push me away from
where I stood so close and bold to the man of the colored
eyes. When the snipping was over, and the women had
wearied of their exclamations and screeches at the sight
of my hair falling around my feet, it was time for me
to make more history.

They gasped, even that ugly boy gasped, for I took the
silver thing from the hand of the tall one, feeling fire
between our two fleshes, and held between my unthink-
ably bold fingers a strand of the limp hair on his head.
The sun reeled in its place and the uncles got to their
feet on the dune behind me, but the tall man obligingly
bent his head down so I could have chewed on his large
nose.

The thing did not work in my hands at first, and after
a few false starts he took my hand in his to show me
how it could be made to cut. Then, amid the cries and
sighs, the clucking tongues and snorts and giggles of the
uncles, aunts, sisters, brothers, and Warra, I snipped at

the hair of the stranger until there were patches on his head where the pink scalp showed through. Then he ran a hand over his head, revealed now to be more or less the shape of all other heads, and straightened up: he was still tall, but not as imposing in the sun now that his hair lay around his feet. I had taken his thing in my own hand, turned it against him, and stolen a little of his power.

There it was, history made on a dune. But my moment was brief: I had only just begun to relish it when Warra cut it short. There he is, striding between the pale stranger and the woman who had been so bold, and he is snatching from between them the shining thing, and flinging it with his powerful spear-throwing arm far into the deep roiling waters of the Wattamolla.

There was a sigh then like the first breath of a storm through treetops, and all of us stood blankly. The tall one stood like a plucked bird, his large hands empty by his sides, and I stood feeling gooseflesh on my skin. Even Warra was abashed after his moment of glory, and stood as ungainly as a few snapped sticks.

It was the ugly boy who moved first to mutter something slyly to the small one. He nodded and spoke to the tall one, who sighed and spoke back gloomily. The sound of his voice made Warra bold again, and he seized me by the shoulder—it would have been by the hair if there had been enough left on my head—and forced me away from the strangers. I could manage only one backward glance before he grasped my chin and turned my head away: I shrieked farewell to the witnesses of my moment, but heard no answer, only the unsteady roar of waves against sand, and the whistle of wind in dry dune grass.

JOAN

I was a woman now, and ripe for history: or if not history, at least some muddle of flesh against flesh. But that bald father of mine was always too strong for me, guarding me against my own flesh, recognizing its hunger, and behind his guarding I remained, reluctantly, virgin territory.

Father knew when I was expected to be intelligent on a bench at the university, taking notes and having my mind improved by the great men of the past. *Hurry, Joan!* He would stand at my door, watching as I dawdled in front of my reflection in the mirror, and in his anxiety his mouth would form the slippery old words of another country. *Hurry, you will be late, the philosophy is at nine o'clock.* So under his scrutiny I would tie my hair up in a scarf and hurry out past Mother smiling her baffled smile, watching her tall daughter swinging her bookbag in a dangerous sort of way.

After the lecture I could never be sure that I would not see his gleaming head among so much unruliness of young hair, and have him take me by the elbow, practicing his best English, saying rather more loudly than necessary in his desire that everyone should recognize his grasp of idiom: *Come on Joan, we will have some bites to eat, I know this part of town like the back of my head.* I would be willing to hurry away with him because, although I loved to be stared at and be the center of some sort of spectacle, I like the spectacle to be of my own making.

He knew, of course, that I had dealings with young men in the lecture halls and libraries, but he dismissed with a shrug those he saw. At home, when he spoke seriously after dinner of my future, he did not speak of purity, or incorruptible vessels, and even less of respect or virtue. *They have no prospects, Joan,* he said. *We came here, your mother and I, leaving our home, only for the prospects.* He relished the whole idea, swirling the whiskey and ice in his glass and placing a tweed elbow carefully on the arm of his chair, a man whose prospects had blossomed and left him a man who could buy the best whiskey and the best tweed as a matter of course, and the best future for his daughter. I knew the kind of prospect he had in mind for me: I was a woman, so my prospect was to be a wife. Oh, I might be the wife of a doctor or Member of Parliament, a lawyer or a Professor of English Literature, but my prospects did not include becoming any such sort of thing myself. I had heard of women, just one or two, who had become doctors and lawyers (though none had so far become Members of Parliament or Professors of anything at all), but they were women of inhuman strength of brain and character, women with a singleminded earnestness of purpose that made them not care that they were regarded as freakish and suspect: they were willing to forgo the love of men, and the possibility of domestic bliss with a brood of laughing children, in order to follow their lonely paths. I knew I was not one of those women. I was not strong enough in brain or in character: I was weak enough to want love, and not to be a strange object like a talking dog. And I liked men, wanted to know their hands on my flesh. All the same I did not relish what my father had in mind for me. *I am my own prospect,* I told him, and heard my voice loud and nasal, as foreign as possible from the smooth outlandish English of which he was so pathetically proud. I did not quite know what I meant, having no image of an alternative to the one he had in mind for me: I spoke out of thin air, out of nothing more substantial than formless hope, and I could not hope to convince him of what I myself was so unsure about. He laughed, thinking me a girl of spirit who would make a fine fiery wife and an electric exclaiming kind of mother when the time was right, and he cared only that I should remain intact.

In the meantime, he could not care much that I cut my hair off in a way that outraged the pink-faced wearers of broderie anglaise, and dyed it every different color that the frowning chemist could offer me, so the unintended final result was a sort of shot green: he did not even care very much that the scarf I tied around my head, making my mother smile nostalgically, did duty later as a blouse, tied precariously around my flat chest. Father was still too foreign to know just how eccentric all that seemed, here in the land of the Angles and Saxons with their pinks and mauves and polka dots, and Mother could not see me either, lost as she was in her dreams of somewhere else altogether.

She smiled gold at me and drifted into soft-eyed memories. *Forests,* she said wistfully. *Trees, with leaves, and mountains everywhere and water on black rocks.* Mother's mouth became thin, squeezed, lemony, suppressing longing for her native land. *And the snow!* she sighed, but Father had a short fuse when it came to waxing lyrical about snow. *Fiddlesticks!* he exclaimed. The English word set the ornaments rocking, and my mother's mouth lost its lemony look as she remembered she was in a new country now, one in which bald men such as her husband became wealthy and plain girls got educations.

When Father did not appear at the university to whisk me away, I passed what he would have called *the times of day* with the people I was beginning to know. The place seemed full of gormless girls like those I had been to school with, who turned the pages of their books only by the corners, and sat down the front of the lecture halls in their practical cardigans. There were young men, too, just as flabby of spirit, who looked startled if you spoke to them, and frowned in the library at the way my bold soles sounded on the floor.

But Lilian, for example, was not one of the gormless ones. Lil was a gigantic person of some boldness, who could be persuaded to laugh with me at the cardigans, and although she looked aghast at what she was doing, was only one step behind me when I took a short chilly stroll among the draped corpses of the medical building. Oh, what a pleasure to have a companion who was also a person of possibilities! Lilian was from some sort of nice home in a leafy suburb by the water, with a respectable father, a ladylike mother, and a lifeless brother. But she was transcending such beginnings: she was a fit companion for a woman with a future.

There was an old rowing boat at her house in which Lil and I pushed off towards Chile and to other adventures. With Lil on one oar and me on the other, so the boat was all lopsided in the water, we did not get very far towards the El Dorados of the Americas, but we indulged other kinds of exploration. That cold green water, into the depths of which I stared until I was dizzy, enticed me to some kind of madness: I felt myself drawn down into it in a kind of swoon. The dazzle of sun on the water and the rude cries of the gulls heated an excitement within me until I seemed about to burst. *Oh*

Lil, I must plunge in! I cried, and while she stared, I stripped the garments from my body and in skinny flesh-less nudity I dived in.

I gasped at the cold and at the pulse that throbbed between my legs, and was confused into wanting to weep and shout at once, so powerful and strange was this feeling buried in the center of myself. It was a kind of delirium, and even when I climbed back into the boat I was still filled with ecstasy like an itch. Lil stared and I was moved to crave the creamy vastness of her body: I fell on her soft mounds and bunches, stripping the clothes from her, consumed with a craving to feel my flesh against another's, to join skin with skin. She struggled, the boat tipped and sloshed, she cried *No! No!* in a feeble unconvincing way, and even as I cried back *Yes!* and wrestled with buttons, I was impatient at her coyness. Where was the spirit to match my own, that could stand naked, shameless and throbbing under a yellow sun, and lust for more?

Lil revealed at last was a pleasure. *Ah Lil,* I said, *this is more like it,* for, free of the ugly rucked-up straining-at-seams clothes into which she forced her flesh, she was a mountainous beauty, her flesh bunched in warm rolls around her person like another layer of clothing. Her body, when I lay beside it in the boat, moved me to tears and to touch its enormous warmth, and Lil was silent beside me, her face turned away up at the sun, her eyes closed as if pretending she was not really there.

Such delights were enough pleasure for some days, but there were others when I was seized by a hunger nothing could satisfy, and I crammed my mouth with my fist and fingers till I was almost sick, and was choked with impatience at Lil and her soft flesh. For I knew, as that gleaming father of mine knew, that it was a man I wanted, and a man I would have.

It was with Lil that I met Duncan, in a lecture hall
stifling with dullness, where history was being spoken of
but would never be made. I saw at once that Duncan
was not one of the gormless ones, and I shook his hand
across Lil's lap so hard I could feel the bones and the
callouses on his palms. While the man in tweed down
below us kept losing his place in his notes, the three of
us enjoyed a few whispered bits of disrespect about Na-
poleon and other subjects, and when at last the man in
tweed closed his notes and we were free, Duncan stayed
with us. He stayed with us on a bench under a tree, and
I stayed, and in the end we outstayed Lil, who went off
with many backward glances and waves while Duncan
and I shifted closer on the bench to fill up the gap she
had left. *Bye-bye Lil,* Duncan called, and *See you tomorrow Lil,* I called, and we watched her enormous
bottom as she walked away across the quadrangle: then
he and I got down to the business of knowing each other,
for we had taken a bit of a fancy at first glance.

Duncan, I discovered, was a secretive roisterer: not a
man of aplomb at all, rather diffident and bumbling, but
also a man of knowing ways with sly fingers in the
interstices between flesh and fabric. *It is us country blokes,*
he said when I wondered at his boldness. *Seen a lot of
the birds and the bees and all that.* Duncan would have
been a rounders player of primness and flat pink face if
he had had the misfortune to be born a woman, because
he was a member of the pallid race that had invaded
this country, and was the heir to unthinkable numbers
of acres and cows somewhere in the dry inland. But he
was no jelly of a man, as so many of the privileged ones
seemed to be: together we had many bold adventures of
a small kind.

With Duncan, I drank tea in cafes down by the wharves,
where sailors in pairs glumly ate burnt chops: sometimes

foreign sailors, with pompoms on their caps, or with flesh as dark and wrinkled as a patient weather-furrowed rock. I loved the black gleam of such outlandish skin, and I wondered if my destiny was to give myself over to the caresses of such a one.

Or we would wander the streets of the Chinese, where the air smelled of cabbage and mice, and wafts of incense from inside dark private doorways, and we were the tallest people in the street. I did not lust after the hollow-chested Chinese youths as I did after the muscular black ones, but was excited to be here, where every closed shopfront could hide an opium den or a harem of slaves, or melancholy lepers hiding from the light. Anything was possible here, even in the food, which was unrecognizable shreds and bits of things: it could have been dog or rat or stewed rope, but I liked it, and knew I was happy when I saw myself reflected in a fly-specked mirror with Chinese writing around the sides, being deft with chopsticks and coquettish with this brave youth Duncan, to whom I was approaching more and more closely, emboldened by him as he was emboldened by me.

Joan, you are returned late, Mother would exclaim at me in an agitated way, showing those gold teeth of hers in her fear. *He is waiting for you,* and there behind her in the living-room I would see the dome of my father's cranium as he waited to hear me explain what I had done that had made me late, and with whom. I did not go into details of young men or Chinese streets or wild-eyed sailors, knowing that Father would not value any of these as I did, and could not be expected to understand that I had a destiny to uncover, although he understood that young men were what I was fancying.

Something had to be said now to explain my absences, which were longer and longer, and at times of day that might have been suggestive, had any suspicions suggested themselves to him. It was one of my jobs to forestall the suggestion of any such suspicion, and my solution was the one that generations of deceivers have used.

Necessity was the mother of the lie. *I have been studying in the library, Father,* I would tell him, or more cunningly: *Elise Cunningham invited me home for tea, Father.* Father nodded in a satisfied way, for he read the society pages like the Bible of this new land, and knew that Elise Cunningham *came from money,* and even better that her family was *on the land* in a big way, and best of all that Elise Cunningham had brothers of an appropriate age to be *prospects* for his daughter. He did not know, and I was not going to tell him, that Elise Cunningham thought Joan Redman might be *a little on the grubby side,* and most certainly that this outlandish girl with yellow skin and green hair and an outrageous scarf tied around her flat chest was not anyone she would ever consider inviting home to tea.

Lilian was the best lie of all, because she was the truth. Father could nod in approval, hearing of Lilian's wealthy and respectable family, the position of the Singers in society, and the fact, and in this case it was a fact, that Lilian Singer, person of prospects and possessed of a brother, had invited his daughter Joan home to tea and to take a turn on the harbor in the boat. When Father's skull gleamed in a suspicious way in his chair and his eyes became small in their intensity, and proof was needed, Lilian could be brought along as large and indubitable proof that I was not, in this instance, lying.

Father did not know, and I was not going to tell him, that Lilian's father, although so respectable when you described his position in the world, was a man of crazed tiny eyes and gigantic hoarse voice listing facts and figures, her mother was an imbecile with the vapors, who could barely gather enough grey matter to remember her daughter's name, and Lilian's brother was a poor spindly damp boy in glasses who seemed nervous of his own feet and hands.

Father knew none of this, and could have *wool put across his eyes,* as he would have said. He was the innocent, and what I felt for him was pity, seeing him believe me, but also something like fear. There was a power in my lies that seemed larger than the words I was handing him, as if I was dealing with an explosive that might take my head off if I became too confident. But my feeling was that, although my manifest destiny remained shrouded to me, I had to make a beginning with it, and the beginning that seemed to offer itself was to follow the voice of my skin. The voice of my skin had no clearer idea than I did of what prospect I should be seeking, but when I inhabited my skin, and allowed it to flame against another's, I was filled with possibilities in a way I was not when I was merely the prospect of a wife.

Joanie, Joanie, Duncan whispered in the dusk behind a bush of the Botanical Gardens. *Your body is pleasing to me,* and I had to laugh at his prissy way of saying that he was huge and greedy in his pants. *It is late, Duncan, I must get home,* I said, but this bush was an old friend, and the grass beneath us was warm from an afternoon of our bodies against it, so it seemed too difficult to move. Everything was humorous now, with the bottle empty beside us, and the guardian of the gardens was a great joke, walking by swinging his lamp and never spotting us. *Oh Duncan, you are a caution!* I told his ear under its gingery hair, and felt him laughing, for he was teaching me how the country folk spoke, and enjoyed the way I did not believe what he told me about what it was like there. *We get on like a bushfire, Duncan, and you make me as happy as a box of birds,* I whispered, crushed against him, feeling his breath pant against my cheek.

And you, Joanie, are a wonder, Duncan said, and slid his hand smoothly between my thighs. I slapped his hand but he, the animal, laughing and transparently sly, removed it from my thighs only to slide it into my blouse, between flesh and undergarment, in a single smooth action that demonstrated that he had been that way before. *Duncan, you will be the undoing of me,* I said, and although Duncan was busy with a nipple between fingers, he was not too busy to say: *Joanie, all the undoing is already done.* It was true, for now my nipple and most of my left breast filled his hot soft mouth, his spiky hair tickled my chin, and there was nothing in the world but flesh against flesh.

Of course it was Duncan who penetrated that ravenous flesh of mine at last, and made a woman of me. My body did not seem to need to learn any trick of pleasure, but was my sly guide into every cranny and crevice of lust. Where had I learned so much? *You know a lot, Joanie,* Duncan whispered later as our flesh cooled together. *Do all the girls know so much, back in old Transylvania?* He fingered my body as if to memorize it, and said, *Joanie, you did not come down in the last shower.* I had the right answer for him, quick pupil that I was. *No,* I said, *I am not still wet behind the ears, or green around the gills, or a brick short of a full load, either.* We laughed so loudly from behind our bush that a startled cat leaped in fright from a tree and ran in a hounded way across the grass into the darkness.

There it is then, I told myself and the stars, and the heavy head of Duncan now asleep on my shoulder. *I have done it. I have become a woman. I am known of man.* It was comforting to tell myself what I had done in such rotund and respectable phrases, for I was feeling weightless, shadowy, marginal, lying on sharp nasty twigs among a smell of where someone had been taken short in a serious way and feeling bruises and aches in parts of myself that had never before been subjected to such stresses.

Joan Makes History

SCENE FOUR

By 1839 free European settlers as well as convicts
were taking root all over the continent. I, Joan,
was there as more and more land was being put
behind fences and under the plough.

U NLIKE so many in the new land, I had not been thrust here without choice, but there had been too many glum hungry winters back in the cheerless Old Country, so that I had sickened of the struggle, and had chosen to leave the world I knew, where things grew worse each year, and to take the great leap over the oceans of the globe. I had leaped up on the back of the great blind galloping horse of history that tramples the weak underfoot, and seized my destiny in both hands.

There were those on board the ship who would have liked to join themselves and their destinies to me. One in particular, a young man of carrot-colored hair, was also being urged over these waves by the thirst for adventure and the memory of an empty stomach. Like me, he was determined that his future would not be like his past, and he hoped for great things.

Jim muttered and blandished, and held my hand so tightly I had to pull it away and laugh at his disappointment. *We would make a fine couple, Joanie,* Jim whispered, but I did not think I was ready to be any kind of couple yet. *Oh no, Jim, I am out for a bit of a lark, I am after excitement and a new life,* I exclaimed into his smiling face, but Jim, with his sandy skin, and the freckles lying along his cheeks like pollen on a petal, did not believe that I could turn him down.

On that day when a low green land to starboard was being examined in silence by everyone massed on deck along the rails: on that day, when excitement and fear were in the air, Jim found a corner where he could take my hand, blush, and mutter a few words about *Going forward together, Joanie.*

Let us cut a long story short, omitting a hundred and one intervening tales of arrival, and the tricks played on us innocents by those waiting for us, so that we quickly became innocents no longer—but let me leave those tales untold!

Let me show you a small plot of sandy land covered with gum trees and small prickly shrubs, down where the explorers had enthused over the land they had subdued to trigonometry. What was neat on their maps, and wondrously promising, was to the naked eye somewhat less enticing. Tall pale stands of straight gums grew like gigantic weeds, spearing up and then branching into untidy bunches of leaves, and bushes of all kinds made it impossible to stroll as they had somehow implied they had. But morning sunlight between those trees was soft: birds trilled and whistled in a secretive excited way, and those odd flat leaves caressed each other against sky as clean as a china plate.

I grew to love those gums in the mornings: I loved the sinuous massive way their trunks rose up into the blue, and the way the bark hung off them in long feathery strips, exposing the solid white skin beneath. On those mornings when the smoke from the breakfast fire hung blue in the air, I walked among them and touched each trunk to feel its cool flesh.

But later in the day I loathed them, when I had to chop at the hard dense wood that was as dry and unyielding as stone, and as heavy. Horizontal, those slender trunks were hateful, bleeding brown sap and resisting every effort with crowbars, wedges, and saws. At night I could feel muscles twitching in legs and arms, and lay dreaming of endless heaving effort, levering a log along the ground to be laid across another, and even in my dreams I clenched my mouth with effort, braced my shoulders and back, and felt pain streak up my legs from thrusting too hard against that unforgiving wood.

The old hands here had devised a few ways of cheating the bush and those gums of a few gallons of the sweat they wanted to extract from us. *Save a third of your chopping,* one whiskery old fellow directed as he passed along the track to his own bit of ground. *You chop a little ways through the trees in a row, see, then when you fell the one on the end, down they all come tumbling like ninepins, you mark my words.* Well, it sounded good as he said it, sitting behind his horse. It sounded grand, and simple, and elegantly labor-saving, but those foul gums foiled such ingenuity by growing just too far apart, and branching out wildly so there was no ninepin-like trunk to come cracking down, and they twisted and leaped as they fell so that they missed each other, laughing, it seemed, and each one still had to be hacked right through.

That left the stumps. Those stumps! They were so close together it would never be possible for a plough to make any kind of furrow around them. They lingered and haunted, tiresome powerful roots gripping yards of soil and rock in a death vice it was impossible to loosen. There were endless hot afternoons of sweat and blisters and flies coming to suck at sweat dripping off my face into the earth, as I battled with the blind strength of those roots. Like a furious mole, becoming more clumsy in fatigue and exasperation, I chopped and gouged at the earth around the dead roots, chipped and grubbed, scratching out earth and stones in a ring around the stump, always feeling the pick strike yet another branch of root whenever there seemed a straight go at a bit of earth. All this tedious scrabbling went on until at last the stump perched in a hole with its roots branching out from it into the ground.

The fires I lit later around those stumps were a cruel satisfaction: I stood watching the flames of the twigs lick out and blacken that pale dead flesh, dry now: but even in death, and even when dry, the wood resisted and quenched almost any amount of fire. I was willing to think I had not waited long enough for the wood to dry, or that I had not the knack of lighting the right kind of fire, or even that these particular trees were of a hitherto unknown variety, completely impervious to flame. Fury mounted in me as I heaped and heaped dry sticks until, reluctantly, without any satisfying flare and blaze, but smokily, sullenly, the stonelike timber began to char and fall away, and the loathed stumps began to smoulder, sending out urgent plumes of white smoke from their tops like a death cry.

With so much timber, after the scarcity back Home an extravagant embarrassment of timber, you might have thought there would be joy in sawing and planing and chiselling, constructing a snug dwelling and a sufficiency of rustic furniture. But no, that wretched timber would not split straight: it twisted and warped in perverse ways, tearing ragged along the grain. Then it was so hard it blunted the saw, and sharpened immensely the tempers of those doing the sawing, so that hours passed filled with hatred for that clotted, obdurate wood.

However, at last there was a hut of sorts, a hut like those we had housed a pig or two in, back Home: a hut all skewed and lean-to, with not a square corner anywhere, just great crude slabs of that loathsome timber stuck upright in the ground and roofed after a fashion with flattened-out slabs of bark. Our hut was like a tiny Stonehenge, built of such huge-hewn lumps, for nothing could be made small with such wood, nothing made fine, no two surfaces ever made to fit snugly together. The great fissures between the planks were filled with such clay as could be found, and I spent hours trying to smooth and beat the mud floor that was slimy when wet but became powdery dust when dry. In the first rains, the clay washed from the cracks and the bark roof let in water along every crack, so that a painstakingly flattened floor became a quagmire of thick mud full of the heelprints of exasperated feet.

Then I labored over the patch of earth that was starting to appear, like a bright spot on tarnished brass, from the wilderness. Each day I heaved at the soil with my pick, thrust at it with a crowbar, and at last with a shovel when the soil was loosened. Such quantities of stones emerged from the soil that I heaped them in long rows, picturing a wall of stones as we had had at Home between the fields. How tame and easy all that seemed now, what mad luxury it seemed to have a plain bit of earth to dig, and four walls and a roof, and a door that was more than a flap of wood hanging from some bits of leather! *We will have a wall here,* I pictured, and wasted a morning with those stones, but there was some trick to it that I had never learned, having had all my walls built for me long before I was born, before even my mother and father and their mothers and fathers had been born. Some trick there was to keeping the stones clinging to each other, some trick of wedging and geometry against gravity: some trick I did not know, and could not learn now, and all my walls came to nothing more than the long heaps of obstinate rocks that had been their beginnings.

As I dug I teased myself with imagining the cornucopia that would pour out of this sandy grey soil. I sweated and panted, and the moisture gushed into my mouth, thinking of the sweet mealiness of tiny pale potatoes, brought up fresh-faced and surprised out of the earth and popped into the pot, of the succulence of young cabbage heaped steaming on a plate, of the tang of an onion eaten in the hand with a great slab of good crusty bread. Oh, the feasts I had in my imagination! And meanwhile it was pease and weevilly flour, the odd bit of salt pork, and now and again a bit of possum that was foolish enough to fall into the snare.

Seed was the most precious commodity. There were many notions shared with us by the old hands, of preserving it in borax from the ants, of waxing the necks of jars, of tying up the bag with Condy's crystals: of keeping many small stores of it, rather than one large one: even of sleeping with one's arm around it, so precious was that seed. Bought so dearly and hoarded with such care, checked every day against damp and the predations of insects and mice and who knew what other alien seed-snatchers this violent land might harbor: that seed was hope. Its successful sprouting meant life, its failure to sprout meant ruin.

Advice was the one thing that was plentiful. There were convictions announced with the flying spittle of certitude that the precious seed must be planted only after the sun had set, or, from another plausible face passing along the track, only in the full heat of the sun: that it should be planted when the moon was full, or on the contrary that it would shrivel where it fell if planted under a full moon. Then there was the dung man, who in a thickness of foreign tongue explained how to mix cow dung to a paste and pack the paste into empty cow horns (where one would obtain such a quantity of cow horns in a place almost empty of cows I did not ask his passionate Slav face). They were to be buried in alignment with longitude, or meridians, or some such, and brought up under the new moon three months later. Scattered on any desert, this Russian or Rumanian gutturally insisted, this substance would make everything bloom in profusion, would ensure that every single seed would sprout, and would produce potatoes the size of a horse (or was it house?).

Freshly dug, the earth had a dark fertile look. But after the sun—hot even in what seemed to be winter here— had been on it for an hour it was again the somewhat grey, somewhat sandy, distinctly unpromising soil I had kicked at that first day but had decided would have to do. My heart sank then at the possibility that all that heaving and grunting, that chopping and splitting and stumping and burning, had laid bare nothing but a patch of arid dirt in which any crop would wither.

And what crop? I knew only two crops, and had seeds of one: if anything was going to grow here, it would be potatoes. I was no expert, having been too feckless back Home, too disgusted and weary to my heart of the whole business to have paid enough attention. I regretted that now, but in any case this bumpy field that had been wrestled out of the wilderness, with incorrigible holes and stumps, boulders and bald patches: this amateurish field, grey under the foreign burning sun, was so unlike the soft smooth fields of home, that lay so tame and green under cloud or tepid sun, that it was all new in any case.

It is all new, I said to myself, but still I tried to remember a thing or two. *Let the furrows march cleanly up the hill,* I remembered them saying, so when it came time to furrow the grey soil I was careful to plough up and down the slope. *Aye, you'll have a good runoff there,* I imagined Father saying with approval, the sodden nightmare of potato rot being in all our anxious hungry minds back there. My furrows, then, marched up and down the slope, and faced perfectly south. *Ye'll not catch me wasting time and good seed planting on a north slope,* I heard Father's voice saying, full of contempt for my ignorance.

I was careful, then, and stood with satisfaction looking along my furrows, on the slope that faced due south. I had checked it with the compass of a passing gentleman on a horse, who had been obliging enough to tell me I should plant to the north, but I had smiled and known better.

I did not pray over the planting of the seed: I had no wish to pray to a God who had made life one of starvation in the Old Country and of endless drudgery in the new. He was watching over those seeds, though. Ah, Joan, how wrong you were about everything you did, and how much that God of yours was caring for you, to make sure of success in spite of every mistake you made! God sent only the gentlest of rain down on my furrows, which with anything stronger would have become foaming rivulets. He sent only the mistiest, most forgiving sun down on my scarce-covered seeds, which would have parched and shrivelled under anything more powerful and, although even He could not correct my folly in planting on the south slope, He had ensured that the slope was slight enough for sufficient sun to reach the earth.

Every dawn found me awake, my hands clenched, my heart beating loud and urgent in my chest. *What? What? Why?* I wondered, until remembering, I arose from the sapling bed and went out barefoot to look at the field. *Will it be today? Will it be? Will it ever be?* And at last it was. At last, in a dawn made metallic by the crowings and warblings of those birds, under the soft fingers of yellow sun breaking over the crests of the trees, I saw thin stands of green, so vague I had to look away and catch them only out of the corner of my eye, so elusive were they: a blur of pale color on the dark earth, a ghostly film of green. Those seeds, all our hope and our future, our sweat and toil, had swelled and burst with life: our seed had taken root and sprouted, new life had begun.

Our seed? you ask. *Our* hope? *Our* future? Who was there, Joan, with you in that rough clearing among the rustling gums? Who had sweated alongside you, chopping and heaving, grunting and digging, burning and building, and who shared that crude hut that let so much of the elements in? Why, that boy I had met on the boat of course, he of the carrot-colored hair and the intensity of persuasion, who had caught my eye, my hand, and at last my heart. He had not left me, and now together we looked out over our gossamer green, our new life beginning.

JOAN

IT seemed to astonish no one that my fornications and lusts had caught up with me, or only astonished myself. I stared at the bland buttery skin of my belly and spread my fingers over its warmth: it was unimaginable to me that a creature had taken root in there, some faceless tadpole conceived out of a night of laughing and flesh, sprouting within me.

I had ignored, and hoped I was wrong in what I was starting to think, and disbelieved all the evidence, so that of course it was now too late for any kind of remedy.

I spoke to this stranger, this Duncan with whom I had laughed and humped, and who had taken root inside me. I felt him watching me, his face empty and unsuspecting. It was a horrible kind of power, to know that I was about to open my mouth on a few words that would wipe the calmness off his face and replace it with some sort of agitation, though I could not quite imagine what kind. The world could never be the same after I had spoken, and I was in no haste to change the world: I loved things as they were, with Duncan eyeing me with a kind of soft salaciousness that warmed me from within. While I was the only person to know of the existence of another being, that person did not exist, but it was not a secret that would stay hidden for very long, so, although it was impossible to imagine that I would ever be able to find the words, and rock the world to its foundations with them, I knew it had to happen. I was like a reluctant machine, sitting numb in the Tudor Tearooms trying to set myself in motion to say what had to be said.

I watched the edge of the table in its red cloth and ran my chilled fingers along a groove, where the cloth could be made to take on a crease from the pressure of my fingernail. *Look, it is like this,* I said jerkily into the friendly silence between us, and Duncan, who was a stranger to me, but not stupid, seemed to become very still, listening with his whole body, as if he knew the universe was beginning its topple. He waited, but my voice had sounded strange to me, unnerved, unsteady, and I could not go on. There was a long silence in which I ran my fingernail along that red cloth in its groove and listened to the fear beat in my head. At last Duncan stopped my hand and said in a quiet way, *So, Joanie, do you want to have a discussion, is that it?* and I looked at him and saw that he could not guess, and was thinking, perhaps, of discussions of a conventional nature on the subject of futures, and where ours was going, and prospects, and intentions. *No,* I said, meaning the thoughts of such a sane and tidy discussion, and jerked my hand out of his so that I felt him become stiff, waiting. *Yes,* I said, after creasing the tablecloth some more. *Yes, it is like this.* I needed momentum to carry me into the next sentence, but the words died on their way from my brain.

Duncan, that patient man, waited, thinking only of words I might say that he would have an answer for. I wondered if perhaps he knew already, whether his calmness meant he had already thought out this future and knew how to deal with it. Did he know, after all, and was he just waiting for me to speak the words?

Come on, Joanie, he said. *Spit it out,* and I took a breath and ran at the words: *It is like this, Duncan, I am with child.* I almost laughed to hear what kind of quaint antique words I had chosen to break the news, so Duncan stared at a face twisted and writhing with mixed passions of amusement and dismay, and I watched him wonder if I was making a joke in poor taste, or what was happening. I tried to be clearer: *I am pregnant, Duncan,* I said bluntly, and the cold words sobered me, and there was, all at once, nothing to laugh at.

I told Duncan all I knew in the way of dates, and certainties, what doctors had said, and how there was no doubt, and all those mechanical facts about this thing that was happening to us. When he had learned all there was to learn, he sat playing with his spoon in his saucer for a long time in silence. I watched his face bowed over the cup: I could see his eyes shifting in thought beneath his lowered eyelids, and I was struck chill with how little I knew of this man. I knew how to make him laugh, and how to make him pant and groan, and bite my flesh with his sharp teeth, but I could not even guess what thoughts were teeming behind his eyes.

It had started to seem to me that Duncan and I would stay here for ever in the Tudor Tearooms, paralyzed by the inexorable workings of biology, when he reached over the table and patted my shoulder. *Well Joanie,* he said cheerily, *I will take you home now.* He smiled, although it seemed that the smiling muscles did not have their hearts in it: but he took my hand, and walked me home in silence, kissed me on the cheek in the entrance of the flats, and waited to make sure I reached our floor safely before walking out into the night.

As for me, I was paralyzed. I could feel the swift-running silent clock of my body and its guest racing towards their own plans, but somewhere remote from that I remained Joan, woman of destiny, whose life was surely in her own hands? Whose future was surely her own choice to make? Whose great, if vague, plans were surely her own to direct?

I was in the mood for telling, though, and having told Duncan, I now had the task of telling Father, and of course Mother. I chose to tell Father first: the words came more easily than they had for Duncan.

My hairless father watched me, those oiled eyes of his not blinking, as if continuing to listen, in the silence after I had spoken. He could have been considering in what way my lips parted when I was in ecstasy, and what sort of sound I had made when the foreign seed of my paramour had been shot into me. But when he spoke, it was of beef. *He is a good prospect, that boy, although the color of a carrot,* my handsome father said, and smiled a fluid smile at the thought of my vegetable love. *And he is a man of little imagination, I would say, and men of little imagination make the best husbands, you will find.* My father nodded so the light caressed the bumps of his skull, that I had been allowed to play with as a child. *Darling,* he said, and smiled his bald man's exposed smile at me, so the skin on his skull moved, *I had hoped for a little more elegance, more chic, for my daughter, but perhaps it is the responsibility of those from the civilized lands to take these rich orange men in hand.* He smiled tidily at me after this speech, and watching that flawless stone head I felt rubbery, shapeless, ill-put-to-gether, as I stammered, *I did not have it in my plans to marry just yet.*

Laughs come in many varieties, and the one my father demonstrated to me now was of the musical, unamused, premeditated kind. He kept it going for some time, as if he thought my obtuseness needed an extensive demonstration. He was in love with his laugh. He was in love with the way he sat elegantly in his chair, with his black silk sock showing below his cuff, with his small feet in the gleaming shoes tidy beside each other. He ran a hand over his skull and was in love with that too, and the way he could control even that hair of his, that had tried to make a fool of him by falling out and leaving him a balding man, and which he had shown who was boss, by shaving it all off.

But I would not be outlaughed by any bald man. *I have a destiny ahead of me,* I said in a matter-of-fact way to discourage a further demonstration of laughing. *I am to be a woman of destiny.*

JOAN MAKES HISTORY

SCENE FIVE

In 1851 deposits of gold were discovered in several parts of the colony, making many people rich overnight. I, Joan, was not one of them, but I learned about stranger kinds of deposits, and other kinds of mines.

KNIGHTLEY was a man much given to the sly fingering of his private parts. *We will lick this country into shape,* he would cry. *We will even civilize the bloody blacks.* Those who did not know about the convenient hole in his pocket would have been inspired by the transcendent pleasure they could see on his face. But I was the woman whose unpleasant duty it was every once in a while to scrub those trousers in my tub of suds, and I knew about the flesh-fingering holes in his pockets. I stood with my sudsy hands coiled in my apron, drying them between rinses, looking over the rails of the fence at where the man Knightley stood heavily on the earth in his hidden socks (which I knew were also full of holes, but holes of no lascivious intent): I watched him exchanging tales of gold with other men. *Mark my words,* I could hear their words carry through the still air that ate the steam from my copper, *You mark my words, oh my very word, yes.*

Knightley stood with a skinny stranger newly arrived in our town, a stranger with tall tales of California and even taller ones of finding gold in our hills, perhaps in Knightley's very own paddocks. Knightley became heated in his enthusiasm for the idea, although not heated enough to ride with the stranger into the hills and suffer cold nights, stalking elusive nuggets beside chilly creeks. No, Knightley was a man well settled on his acres, with his sheep and his fine stone house freshly built: but he was a blustering boasting bluff sort of fellow, and enjoyed the hyperbole of the skinny man, and the possibility that, after all, there might be nuggets under his very nose, on his own land, waiting to be picked up and pocketed. And under Knightley's bluster and bluffness ran darker threads, for Knightley had gone out on a limb to borrow the money for his stock, and his fences, and his horses: Knightley was a man up to his neck in debt, we all knew that, and a nugget or two would prove highly convenient.

The man from California had evidently not been over-burdened with nuggets on the goldfields there, otherwise he would not now be so skinny and aflame with hope on the back of such a broken-down drudge of a horse. But he blazed with conviction that, any day now, he would return triumphant from his journeys into the hills, with bits of bliss in his pockets that could be held up between thumb and forefinger to admire. *I shall be a baronet,* he cried. *My old horse will be stuffed and put into a glass case!* Knightley, a man with a poor grasp of words, and no way at all with a grand phrase, nodded and admired, and had ample time to waste with him.

Personally, I was skeptical of this man whose sharp finger never stopped pointing toward Knightley's hills and who never stopped promising. Women who wash other people's soiled garments learn a thing or two, and there were curious secrets of Knightley I would as soon not have learned. I was nothing but the laundry woman: I was a down-at-heel person who came humbly to the back entrances of all the grand houses on the hill, and spent my days scrubbing things on a ridged board, my hands growing puffy from the big bar of yellow soap. I scrubbed at soiled collars, cuffs full of gravy, socks full of holes: I poked at bed linen tangling in the copper, and heaved and grunted afterwards, hoisting the dripping sheets up into the sun on the clothes-prop.

Of a Monday I was to be found scrubbing for Mrs Cassell and her household, and of a Tuesday it was the Bigelows' endless pinafores and embroidered bibs, and the lawn nightdresses, full of the smell of mother's milk that could not wait for a babe's suck. Poor Mrs Bigelow seemed fertile to a fault, and I had traced the progress of her fallings (the sudden way there were no rags to wash), her confinements (the bloodied sheets and towels), and the growth of her many infants on her good rich milk.

I am impatient to be on with the main story here, but I will complete my week for you for the sake of tidiness. Of a Wednesday there were the gigantic pantaloons of Mrs Cotterill, who was a widow and liked a fresh table-cloth every other day and clean sheets twice a week, so my Wednesdays were busy, her lines all full of those vast pantaloons that filled with the wind and tugged gaily at the rope while the tablecloths snapped and flapped around them. Thursday was my day at Mrs Ridge's establishment, where no lady had ever set foot, but many females of light laughs and loose lips, and most of the gentlemen of this town, and here there were copperfuls of sheets until I was sick to death of their weight through the wringer, and endless slippery piles of underthings: chemises, slips, petticoats, nightdresses, pantaloons as provocative and unlike poor Mrs Cotterill's as possible: endless piles of slithering tantalizing garments, and not much else, just a few collars if Mrs Ridge's gentleman Norman had favored her with his presence that week. And Fridays, well, Fridays were somber days at the rectory, where cups of tea for the washerwoman were not very forthcoming, and Miss Skinner the reverend's sister inspected every tedious bit of starched surplice and bib and bit of fine clergyman's lace, and counted the wine-stained double damask napkins used at Communion. I did not feel inclined to sing over my scrubbing or enjoy a bit of a joke with Bridget in the kitchen at dinnertime, because Miss Skinner had a habit of gliding up behind people on her silent feet and giving a laughing person a nasty fright.

My Saturday was not my own, but it was at least in my own home, for Saturday was the day I took in the washing of the Purvises, the McElroys, and the Russells, and that Knightley: all optimistic folk, but either not prosperous enough just yet to have my services in their own establishments, or in Knightley's case, being bachelor gentlemen requiring little washing done.

Miss Mary Cassell was a fine neat girl with a part in her hair as straight as a horizon and tiny pale hands. Even in the heat of summer Miss Mary's shifts had never been stiff with perspiration as Miss Anne Bigelow's were, poor red-faced girl who overheated so easily! And Miss Mary's fine lawn and muslins came to me often so clean, with only a brown spot like a penny to show where someone (not neat Mary, surely) had been reckless with a slopped saucer, or once an entire strawberry crushed in the folds of the skirt, when she had sat down on it in some mishap. That strawberry was like a drawing, lying perfect, flattened into the white muslin, and I picked it off and popped it into my mouth, where it tasted so good that Eadith the thin-lipped undermaid saw me smiling into my suds, savoring strawberry, which I did not often have a chance to taste, and not being one to easily tolerate a smile in anyone but gentry, began to snoop and sniff and count garments ostentatiously: five, six, and seven, sure that the smile of the washerwoman could come only from some wickedness or thievery.

Well, Miss Mary was a fine neat girl then, off whose clothes one did not hesitate to eat: so I was surprised to pick up her lilac drawn-thread lawn with the spotted cuffs, and find the sleeve with a great soiling of mud, a smearing of dirt that was stiff on the fine cloth. Now, such smudges and cakings of mud were common enough in my own household, for sure, and I was not surprised that in the case of the Bigelows or the Purvises I had to soak and rub and scrub at such large quantities of garden embedded on sleeves and knees. But I wondered, as I rubbed away carefully at Miss Mary's lilac lawn, musing into the warm suds over this and that, as I was in the habit of doing: I wondered what mishap might have happened to Miss Mary, that this sleeveful of earth was evidence of: a broken ankle from slipping on a patch of moss, or a sprained wrist from stumbling down the terrace steps? I would hear it all later from Cook or even Eadith, who loved a good mishap. Meanwhile in the suds I watched all manner of small tragedies rise and form and froth away again.

Being a thorough worker, recommended from one lady to another for her thoroughness, I inspected the drawn-thread lilac lawn for other stains that my small scenes of violence would necessitate: a large green behind on the skirt if it was a slip on moss that was the problem, a rip of an underarm if it was those terrace steps, or a torn hem if it had been a heel caught in loose stitching: but none of these appeared, and the image that formed more conclusively in the suds was of a young lady lying on her side, with some thoughtful damp-stopper under her skirt, but that left elbow sinking in the soft earth of an expensively tended damp lawn, the elbow joining with the earth as the young lady lay without moving very much, doing something interesting enough to take her mind off her drawn-thread lilac.

99

All else was intact, and there were no holey-kneed stockings, no muddied petticoats, no bloodied handkerchiefs used to staunch wounds or wipe at mud. I hung the drawn-thread lilac lawn out at last in the crisp sun, that gave such a clear edge to everything visible, satisfied that every mark was gone, and watched it dancing from the line, and knew that I was joined in a tiny way to Miss Mary, lying on her side for so long engrossed in something or other.

I sighed into my suds at the end of my thoughts, and I thought a great deal, for although I was a red-handed small-eyed washerwoman with dank damp hair and nothing in the way of womanly graces to flesh out my limp overwashed bodices: although I seemed no one, and could not as much as spell my own name, I was someone, though someone whose name would quickly be forgotten for never having been written down. I was someone who thought things over, as the business of squeezing clothes through suds did not by any means engage the whole of my mind.

I imagined, and signs fed my imagination. It came to me as the weeks passed that Mondays at the Cassells were of interest to me now, because of the signs I was seeing there. I was the only person to see them, and what signs! I saw the lilac drawn-thread become soiled in various places, for all the world as if Miss Mary had taken to lying on grass or in the shrubbery inspecting something for long periods of time, or doing something close to the earth that filled her attention. I saw her in the street in the lilac drawn-thread lawn, for it was a favorite, and indeed becoming to her, and I had stared at my handiwork, though Miss Mary, smiling the blind smile of the privileged, did not see the lanky woman in the bonnet with the red wooden cherries, and would not have guessed that such a one knew her secret.

100

Well, I feel you shifting from one foot to the other, growing impatient with my boasting and mysteries. *On with it!* I hear you say. Let me put before you, then, the signs on which my imagination had gone to work. What else could they have meant, the muddied back of the white spotted voile with the dove-grey inserts, the grass stains on the back of the blue pelisse, the hole in the knee of one of the best Coventry stockings, the rip at its top where it fastened to the suspender, the button missing from the daffodil tulle bodice, the fastening askew at the back of the sky-blue organdy and a glove tangled in among the petticoats, of which the thumb had been torn almost clear off, along with the buttons someone had been mad with impatience to be done with?

While in other households I watched children grow up, fall off swings, learn to eat with a spoon, go through childish illnesses, all without seeing them, but knowing from bloodied sailor suits, suddenly clean pinafore fronts, nightdresses stiff with childish vomit: as I knew all this, I knew what Miss Mary was up to in long grass and damp shrubberies, twisting and tearing, and at last there was a sign more unmistakable than all of that. For, after all, could Miss Mary not have simply become somewhat prone to accidents, slipping on grass and rocks, clumsily tearing stockings and gloves, and producing evidence that the imagination of her washerwoman was misreading? But I could hardly misread this particular evidence, or lack of it: a month passed, then two months, and there was no sign of Miss Mary's womanhood: so that when prim Eadith could not resist, but had to tell even me, the mere washerwoman, that Miss Mary was to be married within the month, and was it not romantic, such impulse and haste and oh, what a perfect gentleman he was: when she told me all this, I smiled into my suds but I was not surprised. I could have told her that myself, lacking only the precise name of the glove- and lawn-ripping gentleman.

But when I knew, I was dismayed, knowing what I did of Knightley and his pockets and socks. I would not have wished such a sly and lewd gentleman on any young lady, no matter what quantities of gold might be found in his hills or what number of sheep he owned. What gold he had found already, that man, mining the interior of Mary Cassell! I hoped he would appreciate the quality of his find.

They cheered, and got their rice ready outside the church, and thought I was a terrible grouch, not cheering with them as Knightley in his topper entered the church, but I knew a thing or two that they did not, and could not bring myself to cheer. I held my reddened hands together, and watched Miss Mary step from her carriage on the arm of her father, and saw or thought I saw tears under her veil, not just from the joy of being the radiant bride everyone said she was, and I tried to meet the eye of that Knightley, to convey to him my scorn for all I knew.

Poor Mary, I saw how pale she was under her veil, even watching from the shadowy side door of the church where I took up my position I could see that: I watched her walk with her father down the aisle towards Knightley, who had pilfered her maidenhead and her future, and from where I stood feeling the stone strike chill through my boots, father and daughter had the look of prisoner and warder, the hand of Mr Cassell gripping his daughter's arm like a piece of wood and steering it towards its destiny. He was a man who did not care about any amount of rasping lace or the wilting flowers sweating in his daughter's hands, the gawky bridesmaid or the shadowy man standing waiting to receive his daughter, but he cared about one thing: that no grandchild of his would be born a bastard.

Miss Mary walked with her head bowed so that the blossom all but fell off her bonnet, and even those who did not know what I did must have seen she was in no hurry to take this one last walk of her unmarried life. She was of course not yet visible to any eye but that of a washerwoman who knew what was what, and perhaps that of her mother, weeping—from joy, the ignorant would assume—into a handkerchief laundered and starched and ironed by my good self, and now receiving a mother's bitter tears. The dress, all that blinding white, was of an old-fashioned cut, surprising in such a modern young lady as Miss Mary, but those nodding matrons in their ruffles would have agreed the loose high-waisted fashions were more romantic and more modestly becoming to a young girl than the nipped waists and pert bosoms of the latest mode.

There was the bride in her lace, and all around her was family, blocking every exit from what was about to happen to her: there were the sad plain bridesmaids trying to look optimistic (and if only they had known how all too easy it could be, and how after a certain moment there was no turning back!), clutching their bunches of flowers, there were the matron of honor, the pageboy, the flower girl, the best man, all those smiling people for whom Miss Mary's big day was an excuse for best clothes, too much laughing, and later (for that matron of honor and best man, and some of those desperate bridesmaids), a glass or two to celebrate another life tied up, the knots made fast for ever.

The organ boomed and squealed, silk and taffeta rustled as all the ladies craned to see the bride, and she walked as slowly as if in a dream. I was in the shadows beside the western door, wide open on the sunlit afternoon, and perhaps from my spot there I was the only one to see her falter, stumble, be free for a moment of her father's grip on her arm: saw her look up and out of the door with a wild look under her veil, as if she was about to fling aside her blooms and run, veil streaming out behind her, through that doorway into some different kind of future that did not include Knightley. I saw her moment of choice, but someone else had seen it too: Knightley had sprung down from where he stood with his warder beside him at the altar, and in the moment that his bride glanced out into the afternoon, he had taken her hand in his, not with the grasp of ownership, or the determination not to be made a fool of by any blushing foolish bride: he took her hand in his and tucked it up under his arm as if to cherish it, and they stood like that for a moment while the church was stilled by surprise.

When they turned and took the last few steps up to the altar they were already a couple, their skins warming each other, their flesh connected through palms, and I watched them standing close. The shallow words they spoke while Mr Skinner held his book and prayed over them were not their wedding: they had joined themselves together in that moment when their blood had spoken together through their palms and made its own kind of promise, better than any their mouths were making.

JOAN

DUNCAN had promised it would be dry, and it was: it was all as dry as a dream, and sounds vanished into this indifferent air. I looked for trees, for grass, for flowers, even for weeds, and found none of them: I looked for faces I could speak to, and charm in the way I knew, with my conspiratorial smiles and sympathy, and found only faces like dark gnarled wood in the shadow of thick hats, and women like the fat floury scones they were so proud of.

I saw now that the dryness of sandy Duncan, which had been exotic to me in the steamy fleshiness of the city, was what was normal in this place, and his lankiness and his freckled lizard qualities fitted in here, where the air was so thin and dry there was hardly enough of it to breathe, and it made me dizzy with its buzzing nothingness. Duncan, suddenly substantial, was no stranger, but he seemed strange to me, here in his world where I was the one who did not seem to fit. But he was no stranger to me in the nights, in the gigantic bed we were allowed now that our knot had been tied.

Joanie, can I make you happy? Duncan asked, one night when we sprawled, sated, under a sticky sheet, and the question surprised me into silence, because I thought

107

my pleasure had been obvious. In fact I had wondered, in those silent nights with only stars and space outside, how far my cries of bliss might be carrying, perhaps to the outbuilding full of those men in hats who did things with bits of wire and horses, or perhaps even as far as the dry river bank where the black folk lived. Did they all wink at each other by their fires, and did those skinny-shanked black women laugh so their loose breasts shook, hearing the excesses of pleasure to which their boss was inciting his sallow wife?

You know you make me happy, Duncan, I said at last, in a suggestive way, and squeezed his bump of nipple. He lay silent, and I wondered then if I had misunderstood, or what more it was that he somehow wanted. *Do I not make you happy, Duncan?* I enquired at last, but felt a pulse of indignation at having to ask, for was it not I, Joan, whom Duncan possessed: Joan, charmer, sensualist, wit, woman of destiny? What kind of dullard would it take, not to be made happy by such a person? *Yes, Joanie,* Duncan said on a sigh, and took hold of the hand playing in the vicinity of his tool. *Yes, but that is not quite what I meant.*

I lay feeling rebuffed and wanted to cry out: *What else is there to mean? What else can there be but skins together?* But around the edges of my being there was a fringe of chill, and for the first time I began to doubt myself, and to wonder if there might be something I did not know about, that this simple man Duncan understood, something to do with happiness, something beyond skins that I had no inkling of. I was dismayed: I had always thought myself whole, more whole than most others in fact, but I was recognizing now that there was something that I, Joan, might be lacking: I did not know quite what it was, but I could feel it, a hollow or pocket within my being, full of void.

But I was born to make history, I tried to remind myself. My formless destiny swelled and swirled within me, a great restlessness, a gnawing like hunger: I wanted to make history, although I knew I did not want to explore the Amazon or go to the moon. I knew I could do none of those things, and did not especially wish to, but I knew also that I did not want to be left out of history.

Duncan lay now with the sheet round his cheeks like a nun, smiling in his sleep in a way that could have softened me, if I had watched too long. He was a sweet sleeper, full of innocence and heavy trusting warmth, and I lay awake beside him often while he slept, because my destiny worried me in the long nights when I felt it sliding away from me, out here in this empty land that could swallow any amount of human ambition.

In the morning, Duncan woke to serenity: his eyes smiled when they opened and saw me there beside him, and his arm, still heavy with sleep, held me tightly even before he was fully awake. *I never thought to be so much in love,* he whispered with his eyes soft on me. *I would have thought it was just words.* I knew I would never again meet with a love like his.

How could I tell him that I was in a foreign country under his arm and eyes, not close at all, but hemispheres apart from him? Even I, Joan, had never been able to watch myself as I slept, and I hoped that Duncan never had, for I had a suspicion that my face creased into discontent, and frowned at all the images of my sleep, all my anxieties at history not yet made, and all the unhappiness or boredom: because in the mornings I felt myself as cross and crumpled as paper, lying stiffly beside my husband.

Deception ran deep in my nature like seepage, and it hardly crossed my mind that I could share my thoughts with Duncan. I could live in his country, and even sometimes love the way the leaves hung in bunches from their branches and the way the dappled shade in the glare of midday made everyone smile. But I could never belong to it in the way he did, although I had to pretend to: I could never shed my carapace of deception. I had to wait passively while another creature fed on my own blood, and had to fight myself not to be stifled by panic, the panic of having had my destiny nipped in its bud, and of having had my history prematurely snatched away from me by this tiny thief within.

I was a prisoner of the tadpole inside me. I tried to see this life as my destiny, this history as the one I would make, and to be pleased with being Duncan's wife, and the mother of a tadpole. But I knew in my heart that I could not accept such a place, in the suburbs and far-flung colonies of history.

There were times when I thought it must all be a mistake, in spite of the way my buttons would no longer do up: I could not believe in myself bringing forth a son or daughter I would have to learn to love, who would be attached to me then, by bonds of spirit, forever. I read the books that Father sent me, but did not believe that I would open asunder and force out that alien person from my body. As for all the rest, the fiddly paraphernalia of bootees and tiny garments and nappies; I spent my days in a stupor of refusing to think about such things, and when Mother and others sent such bits and pieces I put them in a drawer and did not look at them again. I did not hate the person within, but as far as my imagination could go, there was no such person.

At other times it seemed terribly real, and I was panicked. Buttons and belts, and strange flutterings, and overweening cravings for fresh strawberries, told me that it was all in fact happening. I was overcome with confusion and wanted to exclaim *Stop! It is all going too quick and I am not ready yet!* and I had a mad feeling that if only I could step out of time and place for a short spell, and collect my thoughts, it would be all right, but I was being bundled headlong and all awkward and unready into this thing.

Letters arrived sometimes: Father wrote regularly to tell me a few facts about cattle and what good prospects there were in them. How he loved the names of cows, never knowing or caring that, out here in what seemed desert, most of the fat-uddered milky beasts he read of would crumple and die within a day. *Santa Gertrudis,* he would write, his elaborate European writing making the names exotic. *Aberdeen Angus, Belted Galloway, Blonde d'Aquitane.* Pouring over the glossy colored pictures in his books on cows, he would not have believed these skinny wild creatures, that did not amble over grassy fields as he imagined, but galloped, lean of shank, over acres of dust and a few desiccated drab bushes.

Poor Mother did not often write, knowing as she did that, although my tongue remembered a few rusty phrases of her language, my eyes could make no sense of it on the page. It was grief to her, I knew, but only part of the larger grief of life, that she had somehow never been able to learn the ways of the new land, and had had to watch her daughter grow up a stranger to her. Mother sent me postcards, patriotic ones of ships flying the Australian flag, or various sepia Sydney monuments: St James's Church, the Customs House, Central Railway. *I hopes you are good,* she would print carefully on the back. *Joan, do not do no runing. Also too much in the bed.*

Lilian surprised me by finding me and sending long scrawled letters. *I am in the loony bin,* she wrote, *and think of you often, Joan. Tell me, do you have a lot of sky there?* I showed poor loony Lil's letter to Duncan, and he frowned and was silent. *There was something up there,* he said at last. *Something went cockeyed for Lil, it is a bad thing, and she is no more loony than you or me.*

But Lilian's problems and griefs, her looniness or sanity, were too far away, although I sometimes wondered what would have happened if it had been within large Lil rather than lean Joan that Duncan's tiny wriggler had buried itself.

There was nothing here to help me believe or make sense, no one who could take me by the hand, look me in the eye, and make me believe that this was my destiny. Here there was nothing to penetrate my stupor. There were mornings when I awoke in panic, my heart thudding, my fists clenched, and I leaned over the big globe in Duncan's study, spinning it with my palm, faster and faster until Peru and Australia and Yorkshire all blurred together. *World!* I muttered. *You could have been mine!* Or with Duncan's magnifying glass I pored over it, searching out the most obscure place on the globe, on which mine would have been the first foot to tread, or gazed at the wide spaces of empty ocean, speculating on undiscovered lands there, awaiting a voyager such as myself. *I could have had you in the palm of my hand!* And what of those places where there was nothing left to discover: London, Paris, Moscow, Rio de Janeiro, places I had never been to, and would never see now, or not as a footloose woman of destiny, but (if at all) as a wife and mother, bowed down with details of socks and Benger's, boiled water and woollies! What pain it would be to see Samarkand as a housewife, unable to turn into that dark alleyway, that mysterious shopfront, to sit down beside the swarthy gentleman with the bewitching eyes! Oh, better, almost, not to see it at all!

So I whirled that globe till I was dizzy, until it ran like liquid or gas under my eyes, until Duncan found me there and tried to cajole me with promises of *Grand Tours,* and *All the sights,* and *What about the pyramids, Joanie?* I restrained myself, but wished to cry out: *Duncan, you are dear, but to your eyes one country is the same as another!* And I knew that no dark alleys or even bewitching eyes would ever tempt him: Duncan's life was entirely and blissfully a part of this particular bit of the globe, and all others were nothing but tall tales for him.

But oh, mine was not! For me, there was nothing here but dust and monotonous sun, and the drone of flies against screens along every hour of the endless silent afternoons. Those afternoons, how heavy they weighed on me! I could hope for so little from them: just a giggle or two in the kitchen with the girls over our bricklike scones, or the tiny drama of a snake discovered under the water tank, or the flurry when a bit of iron was torn off the roof in a sandstorm. These were the greatest excitements I could hope for here under the glaring blue sky, and of such things I did not think history could be made.

As the endless afternoons wore on towards night, even the black folk fell silent, having slipped away from the white man's meaningless tasks of cleaning things that would become dusty again, and tidying things whose nature was to remain in disarray. When they had vanished down to their river bed for the afternoon, I wandered from room to room, touching things that did not tell me anything, and breathing the lifeless air. I was stifled with the dullness of it, the way my life was passing and history was still waiting to be made.

In the long nights, when things hummed beyond the screens—stars or mosquitoes, I could not tell—there seemed no way to believe the sun would ever rise out of the darkness. And even when that red ball did tear itself up out of the horizon and begin pouring down heat, how would it help? No sunrise offered me much here.

But dawn was my time of dreaming: I dreamed of the destinies I would miss out on if I spent my life here, desiccating like Duncan under this vast sky. I sat on the verandah in the wicker chair that was threatening to take on my shape from so much dreaming going on in it, and watched the luminous east. There was comfort in the inevitability of sunrise, but horror, too, in the way it reminded me of other inevitabilities. I would have liked the drama of doubt, would have liked to go on moulding the wicker chair hour after hour while the sky failed to split open and the sun failed to rise.

JOAN MAKES HISTORY

SCENE SIX

The expansion of European settlement resulted in bitter conflicts between Europeans and the Aboriginal people. I, Joan, was there, and I do not shrink from telling the story.

BURCHETT had come to this dry land as a convict, in rags and scowls, and there were those who said you could still see the marks of the lash on his back and the scars of the fetters on his ankles. He had risen in the world, though, getting his ticket of leave, then becoming an expiree, through the efforts of a doting and prosperous spouse who had followed him to the Antipodes, and by the judicious application of cash to various points of the penal system had freed Burchett within a year. Freed, he had never looked back: he and Mrs Burchett had never been folk to put sentiment above the prospects of prosperity, so they had stayed on here and wheedled a grant of land out of those in charge of such things.

From having been one of us, Burchett had a nasty way with those in his power. He was a man with a mouth like a slit in leather, a man quite lacking the gift of the gab, but his good lady could find a way with words when it was waste with pease that had to be spoken of, or the scouring of some rotten vessel or other, and had a voice like a rasp for such moments.

Burchett, with his watch chain and his bushy whiskers, stood watching as we labored for him. He stood in gleaming boots pointing and shouting, supervising the erection of stone columns for his lions—all the way from England, and an exact replica of those on the gates of Lord Dover of Marchmont—to sit on either side of the iron gates. He stood watching the sweat of his assignees, his expires, his emancipists: he stood legs astraddle, exchanging a few words about the Old Country with other men in whiskers for all the world as if he had not come here in those foul ships at the pleasure of the Crown. With his neighbors, who did not ask too many searching questions about origins, Burchett became nostalgic for roast beef and fogs. They dreamed, all those men, of making this land look like the old one, and tried to ignore the fact that plum pudding in December brought on the heatstroke, and that the barbarous screeching birds had no respect for the British flag, but would rip it to shreds if they got the chance.

The yellow blocks rose shout by shout, and when the columns stood with their lions in place beside the heavy iron gates, there was no mistaking that this piece of dirt, barricaded behind such stone and iron, belonged to someone. The wives of the neighbors came then, and stood about while servants held their horses, gesturing about rose gardens and arbors, *and over there, a lily pond*. After the fine curved stone steps were built to replace the humble wooden ones, men presented ladies with elbows to help them up to the verandah, and at the top they turned to admire everything, and tried not to pant under the silk and whalebone. The shadows of parasols hid cheeks flushed with exertion under a foreign sky. They departed again on their meek horses, calling out to each other about sundials and goldfish, before the flies could discover a way to penetrate their shining sweat-wet silk.

I was there, but not in silk; I was one of those who had hopes of better things in the future, having gotten a

118

ticket of leave and no longer so closely watched. But til I became a full emancipist I did not have much choice and had to bend over washtubs and kitchen fires, and pluck fowl which others would eat. My destiny, at least for the time being, was to bide my time, and my days and cold nights by the kitchen hearth were spent in the company of various folk I would not have chosen for companions.

Sid was a servant and lag like myself, but was as bossy as if he thought himself my better. Sid was a teller of tall tales, tales of paradise in the interior of this land, where herds of wild cattle stood still to be slaughtered, and trees dropped succulent foreign fruit into your hands. Closer to home he had tales with which he hoped to frighten me, of snakes as big as your arm—or was it that they could take your arm off in their jaws?—up in the hillsides of bush that watched over us.

Sid was a man of bad teeth and tall tales which were not even funny, not tall enough to titillate. *You are too short in your tale, Sid,* I had shrieked at him once, after some farfetched boast or other, and he went white, then blotched red, thinking I had spied on him in a solitary moment and was disparaging his privates.

Will was a young man like a doughy damper gone wrong, with tiny creases of features on a white face that looked as though it would take on a dent if you pressed it with your finger. Will did the horses, and was simple, and not particularly willing, except to champ his way through any kind of victuals, and sit with a slack dribbling grin listening to gabby Sid.

I did not like them, and they did not care for me: their eyes flickered over my face, noting every pockmark, every wrinkle, every infelicity of feature, and with each one they loathed me more. My ugliness had saved me many a carnal experience I had no desire for, so I had no argument with my ugly face, but I had spent much profitless time in my life longing to be elsewhere, or someone else altogether, and there had even been days when it had seemed preferable to be any stubble-jawed leering man than a woman as plain as a frying-pan. At such times I knew I would spend my days being shouted at by angry people who, being more beautiful, should have been kinder.

Burchett and his good lady had their land, their servants, their pretensions to glory: they congratulated themselves that, thanks to them, civilization had come to this valley. Civilization was fine stone houses with lions and sundials, it was legs of mutton and tumblers of rum and water, and it was solid fences that left no doubt at all about ownership. All day the valley was filled with the hollow knock of axes against wood as another bit of post-and-rail went up around another square of dirt: a fence gave a man like Burchett the courage to puff himself up and become righteous about thieves and robbers.

By whom he chiefly meant the blacks, of course: the blacks who came to the kitchen door from time to time, grinning in their saucy way and cadging a bit of sugar or tea or flour, exotic delicacies to them. They did not understand about fences, or owning things, and they did not have to labor mightily with hoes to extract a bit of nourishment from the soil, and we, in our unnecessary layers of clothes and our frowning worries about everything, were figures of some fun to them.

They had been here long before us, and had lived here for who knows how long without any assistance from sundials, lily ponds, or stone lions, and seemed to have managed without two sets of themselves, one in chains and one in silk. These folk seemed to have managed, in fact, with no more paraphernalia than one or two carefully chosen sticks to throw or dig with, and with this elementary equipment they did what we could not: they did all right from this unfriendly landscape.

What did they find here to eat, those skinny black folk, in these empty-looking hillsides of nothing in particular? What were they feeding on in the nights, that made them laugh so much? I knew they did not recognize pease as food, which personally I saw as one more sign of their intelligence. We knew about the wallabies, thrown in great chunks onto their fires, hair and all, and once or twice I had felt the juices gush into my mouth, catching a whiff on some cold evening of the smell of singed wallaby hair and roasting flesh over embers. They were generous folk, and sometimes offered us the bleeding flesh, but we were haughty and shy of their generosity.

It was not always wallaby or possum: I had seen them returning from the hunt with other dead creatures, huge lizards—they called them goannas—and things like rats. The bark trays they carried were sometimes full of clam-like things from somewhere—we in our skirts and aprons could never find such delicacies—and there were other times when I had peeked into their trays and seen grubs, fat white caterpillars, bits of berry and roots and the unappetizing-looking stems of some white plant. I had tried pointing and mouthing and miming the actions of eating, but they were too clever to understand, and only laughed with their fine teeth and shouted to each other and laughed all the more.

What could a toad-white invader, spotted from too many pease and skinny from this lean life, do then, but show her own bad yellow teeth, laughing back? I saw them watch my mouth and its rotten teeth, saw them watch my grey face wrinkle when I laughed, and they called out to each other and laughed behind their hands, looking at me sideways as I had looked sideways at the dwarf and the bearded lady at St Alban's with my beau

George, before everything had gone wrong. I had watched
their deformities with just this askance horror and just
this kind of smile, though I had not had the good manners,
as these folk did, to hide my emotions behind my hand.

They were feckless folk, and for their cheeriness the
builders of fences accorded them nothing but contempt
and the suspicion that they were not as guileless as they
seemed. If a sheep was found killed and thrown on one
of their fires, or if a blanket went missing, Burchett grew
purple with outrage, and small bands of men went up
into the hillsides with guns over their shoulders and
retribution on their minds.

Our Burchett was long on retribution, and relished a
bit of punishment. Of a Sunday, after the thin hymns
had been sung, and the Lord of fences and justice had
been invoked, Burchett got down to the business of
judging and meting out punishment. Burchett sat on his
rock, with a few sacks protecting his bottom from the
chill. He judged, and I judged too, sitting on a tuft of
wet grass watching his meaty face catching the light in
an unappetizing way.

My judgment on him was that he was the kind of
person a new country did not need, in spite of his ability
to *open up the land* and *make something of it,* and *bring
the wilderness to heel,* and all the other dubious things
the assistant governor had praised him for, laying the
foundation stone for Burchett's square house. Burchett
sat solemn on his sacks, and beyond the tiny patches of
civilization down here on the river flat, this country
hummed and ticked under the sun, the hillsides all around
us shivering with gums and revealing cliffs, caves, tumbled
grey and yellow rock that had no time for Burchett and
his judgments, or the rest of us pasty-cheeked aliens.
Birds knew what we were, and even Burchett was forced

to delay his ugly words while something jeered from a tree.

But spring was in the air now, and after the judging that morning I could not bear the cheerless muddle of Burchett's empire any longer. After the morning's judgment, even the dread of the birching Burchett administered to his females was not enough of a threat to stop me escaping for an hour or two. After dinner was done, and those who had had enough to eat were dozing it off, and those who had not were dreaming of loaves of good bread, not moldy damper, and slabs of rare beef, I slipped out of the house and up into that strange hillside that towered over all our puny activities in the valley.

I clambered up the hillside, out of sight of our little muddied patch of civilization, into a sweet dry smell of leaves and sun on stone. It was what they were calling the bush, and in spite of flies it was not such a terrible hell on a smiling blue day such as this was, with winter and pease behind me and the prospect now of a fresh carrot soon, or a mouthful of cress. Even this grudging grey landscape had softened enough to throw a few tiny spiky flowers out of some of the bushes: there was a purple one like an outlandish sweet pea, and a red one with a small alluring throat. I sat on a rock and listened to the echoes as Sid called to me to complete some dreary task of drudgery, but I soon tired of his shouts, picked up my skirts, and wandered out of range of their unfriendly voices, climbing past platforms of soft stone and down into the gully of ferns on the other side.

Sid had told of snakes and spiders in the gully of ferns, but it was sweet there with the new spring sun slanting in as if it had just found this place to warm with its fingers, the ferns were jewels of green; there were pillows of moss on stones, and a domesticated plink from water dripping off a bit of rock into a pool somewhere. Sid had boasted of encountering huge snakes here, but what I found as I blundered and marvelled was a person, dark brown, naked, wild of eye, female, in anguish.

She had known I was there long before I had seen her, and gave me no more than a rolling white-eyed glance from her streaming face as she hunched over herself, keening among the ferns and the trickling water. I stopped short, feeling my skirt fanned out behind me, trapped on some thorn or other, and felt my lunch rise bile-like into my throat as I watched this metallic female coil over herself and retch, choking and bringing up long threads of yellow spit. She held her belly with both hands, hugging it, stilling it, crying in pain and something worse, grief and loss, and fell to her knees, still embracing her round brown belly. Then I saw that the gleam and shine on her thighs was not just the polished gleam of her skin, but liquid of the thick kind. I saw now that it could only be thick painful blood, oozing out from between her thin legs and streaming down the skin, although with trembling horrified hands, wailing, she tried to keep inside her what was determined to come out.

I had seen nothing of this kind before, and was myself undefiled by the lust of any man, being lucky in the ugliness of my face, and the strength of my arms in fighting off the clamors and blandishments of men. But I knew what must be happening to this dark woman, and although I was helpless and afraid in this somber gully, not sweet any more but hushed as if appalled, I knew I must approach the center of this terrible event, and share it in whatever clumsy way I could. *It is all right,* I said and kept saying as I approached her. *Do not despair,* and *God is with you and will grant you another.* It comforted me to know that she could not understand the words, so I did not have to try to get them right, I needed only to speak to her fear and pain, of others near, of sympathy, of the caring of one stranger for another in travail.

I heard them laughing when I got back, and was in no hurry to enter the squalid room where the fire would be smoking, choking on itself, and Sid would be knees apart on the stool before it, toasting his hands and boasting of this and that, and I knew that they would all gab at me for vanishing into the prickle for a whole afternoon.

Burchett was speaking out of the slit in his face when I went in with my armful of wood for the fire. For an astonished moment as I stood by the door I thought he was crying, so odd and choked were the sounds he was making. I nearly dropped the wood and leaped for joy, for what was sad for Burchett could only be glad for me. But, clutching at sticks as they began to fall from my arms, I saw that what was happening was stranger even than Burchett crying: it was Burchett laughing, and I saw too that Madam's hard face was also broken up, in a way that was frightening, by mirth.

I felt fear then, because Burchett and his Madam would laugh only out of some wickedness done, and I knew that I would not be laughing with them if I knew what they were finding so funny. I was chilled as I crossed the room through their hideous humor, hearing Burchett say: *See the way they were grinning away, too stupid and savage to know any better.* Madam laughed a raucous laugh like a cockatoo triumphant over a grub in a tree, and shouted in her hilarity: *And didn't they think they was that clever, lifting it from under our very noses!* Chill prickled and goosefleshed me then and I could not leave the room quickly enough, stifled by the possibility of understanding what it was they found so funny.

But out in the cold kitchen, where Sid sat, as I had known, smoking his hands like small hams at the smoulder in the hearth, it was no better, for Sid was gabbing to dull Will, and I was forced to bustle over pease and pork so that I could not escape to anywhere else. No matter what a clattering and banging I produced with pots and pans and iron spoons, I could not help hearing Sid telling Will what I did not want to hear: *Them dumb blacks,* Sid shouted, and Will grinned and goggled. *Three bags of flour they made off with, plenty for all them thieving heathens to go to Kingdom Come and back!*

I could not eat the vile food I cooked that night, could not even make a pannikin of tea go down my throat, clenched tight against the images in my mind's eye. They were all in fine fettle, though, those other human beings I shared my life with, and gorged themselves, knowing the plenty of summer was coming, even Burchett cramming great forkfuls of pork into his mouth until the grease ran down his chin. They ate, and gulped at their tea, and were full of joy, knowing that out among those tiny lascivious flowers, under bushes full of thorns, in gullies of trembling ferns, that woman and her tribe, whose wallabies had made the saliva gush into our mouths, were in agony, with their bellies full of damper poisoned with our hatred and fear.

JOAN

IN the white tight hospital bed I was weightless, my head as airy as something that might float up and out at the top of the window. I had felt light before, on the bed at home waiting in vain for the poisonous blood to stop seeping from me: that had been a lightness of head, yes, but a malevolent heaviness of every limb that made me hardly care when at last they lifted me onto a stretcher and put me down in this hospital bed. No, the airiness I felt now was strength returning along every vein, filling again with that bright blood I had seen altogether too much of: the airiness was having the heavy hand of that particular destiny removed from the back of my neck so I could turn to the left, to the right, go backwards or forwards as I pleased: I was free.

I lay watching shadows move across the wall and listening to the foreign sounds of life outside my window: out there I had seen a red brick wall with dustbins, a sprawled dog with bald elbows, and the amputated-looking limbs of a leafless frangipani: from my bed I could hear dustbins clank, feet walk, the dog bark, children rush and shriek, and the unending hum of the city's life beyond. I lay comforted by life outside my window, that life I would soon join again in my full strength, and I

rehearsed my destinies. Prime Minister! Discoverer of
the atom! Thinker of great thoughts! All these futures
were open to me again now: my mind was filling like a
hole in the sand by the sea, with visions of futures for
myself.

I was sad, too. I was airy from freedom, but also from
emptiness: there were times when they seemed to me to
be hard to distinguish, when my freedom gaped like a
hollowness within me. At those times I choked with my
own lack of substance: I was nothing more than a speck
of fluff lost in air. I was attached to nothing at all: I had
no past, no future, and a present of no importance: my
being had come into existence and would flicker out in
the blink of an eyelid. The universe would not so much
as register that I, Joan, had ever been.

That was fear I could find no words for, only a hopelessness and the isolation of spinning off forever in a
cold void. *I have looked on the face of death,* I reminded
myself pompously. *And would be lacking soul if the experience had not shaken me.* I pulled the chilly hospital
covers up to my chin and tried to think of the sunshine
outside. *Of course I am a little gloomy, I have just now
nearly died.*

As for that other creature, who had looked on the face
of death and been snatched away by it before its time:
I mourned, and was confused by my grief, for it had
never been more than a faceless thing, not a person for
me (I had never, in the end, worked out just what a
matinee jacket was): and even as I mourned, I rejoiced
to be again one person, Joan alone once more.

It was odd, then, to find myself at one moment with
slimy tears running down my cheeks in despair, and the
next to be craning to see out my window to catch a
glimpse of two little girls becoming shrill over the last

chocolate frog. I, Joan, found myself now to be a confusing matter, where I had always before known what was what.

When Duncan came to see me, the garish roses in his hand made his face sallow. I had never before seen Duncan in the grip of grief, had never before seen his face with no laughter in it at all: this man gazing at me, his flowers laid on the bed against my knees, was no one I knew. He sat down on the unwelcoming hospital chair looking at me with a sad stranger's face, and out of a long silence said at last: *I should have looked after you better,* and coughed as if he had not heard his voice for a long time. *I should not have let you do so much.*

What had I done? I had sat, and strolled, and admired sunsets and horseflesh: the most vigorous thing I had done was to mix scone dough in a bowl and laugh myself silly later, taking the rocklike knobs out of the oven. *Next time I will take more care of you,* Duncan promised, and I did not like the sound of that at all: for one thing I was in no hurry to embark on a *next time,* and for another I did not care for the idea of being hovered over and trapped on a chaise longue for nine months, forbidden to do anything of interest.

Fit as a fiddle, the doctor had declared. *Tight as a drum. All shipshape and Bristol fashion.* It was not I who had needed the reassurance, but Duncan, haggard by the bed. *She will be all right, then?* he asked, wanting to hear again: *There is no reason why next time your confinement will not be a complete success.* Duncan's face had lightened, he gripped my hand so hard it hurt, and I had not been able to look into his optimistic face, for the disloyal thoughts of Samarkand blossoming in my own heart. I could see him planning our future again: the insects would continue to hum away in the afternoons out on the property, as they always had, and the scornful birds would continue to taunt with their slow cries of ennui. Heat would shimmer, the roof would creak under the sun: all would be as it had been before, and the idea filled me with weariness.

We will take a holiday, Duncan promised now. *What do you think, Joanie, we will go to the sea, or the mountains, whatever you would like.* But I knew that no holiday was going to cure what ailed me, and I did not reply, taking refuge in my convalescent status to lie and allow the silence to accumulate while Duncan mused.

I could not imagine Duncan's thoughts. I thought he mourned, but mourned for something that had never become a person, and he rejoiced in the idea of a holiday, a time of ease, untroubled by the anticipation of a stranger arriving. Unlike me, of course, he looked forward to the eventual arrival of that stranger, who would join us at some point in the future: it was not he whose body would be host to that parasite and it was not he who would have to lie like someone with the vapors for so long: it was not his beckoning destinies that would have to be forgone.

Imagining all this in Duncan's mind, I was not prepared for the sounds I heard from him now as he sat in the quiet of this room. It was nothing as solid as words: it was small noises of pain like humming, as if he was setting up a vibration in his head so there would be no room for thoughts. *She is gone, she is gone,* he began to whisper at last, and I saw his sandy cheeks glistening with tears, and even I, cold Joan, who was born to make history and not to sway in the blasts of feeling, was shaken, looking at his guileless grief.

It was nothing, I tried to say. *It was just a few cells, it was no one,* although I had seen it, and knew better, but he cried out more loudly then: *No, no, that is not true!* and I was silenced—and rebuked—because in my chilly self I could find none of the passion he felt.

Seeing his rough sandy face distorted by tears, feeling
my own eyes itchy with dryness behind their lids, I saw
in that moment's cold clarity that this man was too good
for me. Duncan was not the man I had thought he was,
slapdash, a rollicker through life on the backs of fine
horses and the fronts of fine women, a cheery shallow
man full of jokes and benign lusts. He was a man of
feeling, a man of heart, more subtle than my shallowness
could understand, a man full of the mystery of goodness,
a man not ashamed to be human. I fell silent in shame,
seeing what an empty shell of a person I was, and how
far removed from Duncan, for all that he was the man
whose body had penetrated mine, and his was the voice
that had sighed into my ear on so many hot nights.

We sat in a long silence, avoiding the sight of each
other. It seemed impossible that our skins would ever
touch again or our eyes meet, for Duncan was lost in
feelings I could not guess at, and I was hollow, lying like
a dry husk on the bed, brittle, rattling in the wind.

Of course it was Duncan who gestured first across the
space between us. He took my hand in both of his, so
that I felt the rough skin of his palms on mine, and the
warmth of his innocent blood, that was making me so
ashamed of how inept I was in the face of life.

He took my hand and crushed it between his and
looked into my face, but I could not meet his eyes. *Joanie
dear,* he whispered, and although I could not watch, I
felt him lift my cold and loveless hand to his soft mouth.
*Joanie, it was only one, we will have another, there will
be another,* I felt him covering my hand with kisses, my
brown forearm felt his cheek soothe itself against my
hand, and at last I felt heat behind my eyes, and tears
there, because I knew that I was not good enough for
this good man, and although he would doubtless become

a father some day, I did not think it was I who could make a father of him.

I could not say anything of this, though, and had to lie bleak and numbed, a hypocrite, congealed with the knowledge that some part of me was missing, or numbed, or stunted, that I could watch so coldly as two people exchanged sounds through their mouths.

Duncan loved me, and I deserved no such thing as the love of a good man. *I thought it was just lust,* I said aloud, surprised to hear my voice vibrating in my head, for I had not intended to speak my thought. Duncan shifted in his chair and his face blossomed into a smile. *Oh yes,* he said, showing his pink tongue, *there has been any amount of lust, too, Joanie, my word yes.* He took my hand but then thought better of it, thinking perhaps I would misunderstand and expect lust then and there, and put it back where it had been lying on the sheet. *You know, Joanie,* he said from the chaste distance of his chair, *Your body has always been like a red rag to my bull.* He sat smiling at me and at his fancy, and although the smile faded soon and left his face sad, I could see that his anguish had lifted now, and he was thinking not of the child he had lost, but the one he would soon make.

Duncan, I do not deserve you, I said, feeling my lips dry, wondering if the syllables were shaping themselves right, or if I spoke that other language of my infancy. I rubbed the back of my hand across my mouth and felt my lips move, and knew that I must have spoken, but Duncan sat watching the flowers on the bedspread, his large hand lying beside them stiffly. *You are too good for me, I am vile,* I said, and took that hand, which did not look warm, but was, full of the warm loving blood of a good man. He stirred himself out of some gloomy dream then, shifted in his chair, squeezed my fingers, and gave me a look that was an attempt at a smile. *Well Joanie, I do not know about that. We are none of us perfect.* He thought for a while and turned my hand over, running a finger along the lines of my palm as if he knew what they meant. *Or we are all perfect in parts, is that it?* he said, and laughed in a sad sort of way.

Not so long before I had been a giddy girl with my life tame in my hand; a giddy girl spinning all alone with ribbons and scarves of infinite possibilities swirling around her in gaudy kaleidoscope patterns. Now, lying here nodding while Duncan comforted himself making plans for us, I saw that all those ribbons were anchored now: I would never again dance with my life on my palm like a jewel: I was attached now to this man, and to the history we shared. I was responsible—I recoiled in the bed from the idea and drew my knees up as a barricade— I was responsible now not just for myself, but in some degree for this other human, who could not fail to be affected by anything I might choose to do.

Now that was a prison!

JOAN MAKES HISTORY

SCENE SEVEN

By 1855, when Britain was fighting Russia in the
Crimea, Her Majesty's colonial government went
briefly and grandiosely to war against a few dozen
tipsy gold-diggers. At this time I, Joan, played only
a decorative part, but I yearned for grander things.

I gave a great deal of consideration to pink during my long dull days, and to mauve, and spent hours contemplating the small grades of difference between these languid colors. With Betty, the gawky maid who was the best this colony could produce, beside me breathing loudly into the wardrobe, I spent long empty afternoons laying out garments, gloves, scarves, and ribbons on the bed and holding them up against my skin, sadly sallow in this heat, and with real rosewater in such short supply here, so far from the Old Country. Vapid hours passed while my palm smoothed the textures of muslin, of silk, of taffeta and cambric, until my skin was weary of so many fine distinctions, and my back ached from the boredom of it all.

The ennui of so many petticoats! The drudgery of dressing on those mornings, when skin and air-smoothed and shaped each other, and it was wicked to interrupt that caress! Oh, the loathsome feel of silk, slimy and clinging, shiny and choking, and the pinch of the rotten shoes on my feet! I had often been told, *Lady Stoneman, what tiny feet you have!* People had exclaimed, and everyone had looked at my feet, and I had thought it was worth the pinching and squeezing to have everyone ad-

139

mire, although why my small bust should be a matter
for tactful glances and insincere consolations and my
small feet a matter of envy was beyond me, if I made
the mistake of considering the problem.

You do not believe that a lady of leisure, the wife of
a governor, a woman with breeding shaping every movement and phoneme, could feel such disgust at silk and
small feet. You think, perhaps, that being bred to a life
of idle chat, it was what I enjoyed. It is true, yes, give
me a horse and damper, or an army of unshaven men,
and I would not have known what to do with such things.
But that does not mean I did not know what I lacked,
and did not dream of all my other destinies.

I was not born for this kind of small beer, I whispered
to myself as I pressed my forehead against the window
and stared out at gardeners fingering their spades, pretending to dig zinnias. *I was born for more than this,* I
whispered, and in the drone of a blowfly up near the
ceiling, where the air hung stagnant with the dullness of
everything, I allowed myself a dream or two of how my
life might have been, had I not become the mere wife
of a mere dull worthy governor of a bleak and cheerless
bit of Empire, where pink and mauve did not matter
and real rosewater was hard to come by.

I could have been—no, would have been—a woman
of wit, captivating every heart, my salon the center of
all that was scintillating. *Oh, she is bold, she is perhaps
a little too forward,* dull women would say, but they
would envy me my purple ostrich feathers, my extraor-
dinary afternoon dresses of outlandish but successful cut,
and most of all they would envy me the brilliance that
made all the fascinating men of the time stare and swoon
and thrill to charm me. I would have had sonnets written
to me, and it would be whispered that I had permitted
one or two of the more ardent poets to hold my throat

in their slender poets' fingers and caress it till I was
speechless. There would have been stories—and, oh, I
would not have denied them—of poets driven wild by
my bewitching charms, and bursting in through the french
doors of my drawing room, their cloaks streaming out
behind them in the hurricane of their passion, flinging
themselves at my tiny slippered feet. *Joan, be mine,* they
would pant, or words to that effect, but possibly a little
more poetic—and I would smile my maddening smile
down at them as they covered my ankles with kisses,
and whether or not I permitted their kisses and their
poetry to rise by degrees to higher points of my anatomy
would always be a secret between them and me, and the
envious gossips with their dull husbands could conjecture
and hiss with malice, but would never know.

Husbands! Well, even I, Joan, would need one, I supposed, to give countenance to my salon, and pay the
bills of my genius of a dressmaker, who could whip
together a little silk and a little brocade and produce a
masterpiece for my body.

Ralph was a good husband, and dutifully admired each
new pink, every mauve, and was man enough to pretend
to care whether my gloves exactly matched the tussore
insert in my bodice, when in fact the poor man could
not tell green from red. *Yes, Joanie, I believe you may
have a point there,* he would say, and would cock his
large bunlike head on one side when I pointed out the
shade's difference between a lilac insert and a mauve
glove laid across it. I had to love him, was forced almost
against my will to love him for his goodness and the
simplicity of his kind deceits, his desire to please. But
my poor Ralph would never know the histories I lived
on the hot afternoons, when he was busy getting irritable
on the back of a horse, inspecting things, and supervising
the erection of his fortress to repel the Russians—histories

in which he, poor doughlike man, had no part to play at all.

Could I perhaps have been another kind of Joan altogether, flat-chested on a prancing horse, speaking French as if born to it (well, I would have been born to it, in fact), leading men into battle behind me, and dying a glorious if dreadful fiery death in the end? I would have loved the flat-chested part (in fact I was already equipped for it) and I would have loved the prancing horse part, and the roaring men behind me, following me to death if need be. But what if the wood were green, in that last event, and my death were one of choking on smoke, my face not lifted serene among the flames, but spluttering and streaming, red and gasping, dying like that, slowly, in disarray? Perhaps it would not be worth the prancing and the roaring for that.

Late in the afternoons, when the shadows were finally starting to lengthen and the blowflies gave up for the day, Ralph would come home, sweaty and silent, with the furrows deep between his eyes. *Ah Joanie,* he would sigh, and lie back in his leather armchair. *Joanie.* He was a man of much feeling but few words, and I had learned over the several years of our marriage that when he said *Ah Joanie* in just that way, it meant he was glad to be home in his leather armchair, and glad to be with me, and I knew that if I came over and stood behind him, and smoothed those furrows on his forehead, he would close his eyes and smile his inward-looking private smile. Ralph was a better man than I deserved, though, because even as he smiled and I soothed, I was dreaming of leading armies or droves of inflamed poets.

I knew other women had their secret lives, too, and there were times, with the other ladies of quality in this colony, when we tittered over the tinkle of teacups in saucers, and from below our fine eyebrows, and above

142

our charming smiles and dimples, we would exchange a
glance or two that said we knew, and shared, and were
in the secret together.

They are so terribly INTREPID! Mrs Beauman exclaimed in such a languid drawl it was droll enough to
make us all laugh. *So frightfully MASTERFUL!* Mrs
Beauman did not bother with petit point or tapestry-
work while we sat over our tea and titters: Mrs Beauman
reclined on my best brocade, taking her ease, and loved
nothing better than to make us laugh at our menfolk.

My William, she said in her droll weary way, *do you
know, my William cares so much about things, he has
been known to burst the buckles right off his shoes, caring
so much.* Mrs Beauman arched her fine eyebrows and
rolled her eyes to the ceiling, but did not otherwise
interfere with the plaster perfection of her face. Somehow
Mrs Beauman, as well as having been endowed by ca-
pricious Nature with a large and shapely bust, also had
the secret of resisting sallowness in this foul climate, and
had some secret source of rosewater, I was sure. Mrs
Beauman seemed to have no great need of consoling
histories invented in the drone of afternoon flies. Somehow she was someone who was already not quite true
to life, someone I found the slightest bit alarming as I
watched her watching the world from her fine eyes. She
made us laugh with the words that came from between
her somewhat thin lips—I saw now that her lips were
somewhat too thin, and pouted my own out fuller, in
consolation. If Mrs Beauman made histories for herself,
in the privacy of her chamber, surrounded by a boring
bedful of her blues and greens—no feeble mauves for
Mrs Beauman, I was sure—they would be far more outrageous, and more satisfying, than my puny ones.

There was something I wanted to say to these women,
something unspoken I would have liked to share with

them, these three wives whose husbands were out in hot
thankless scrub far away, rounding up wild gold miners
shouting about democracy. To Mrs Henry Miles, Mrs
Stanley Peeper, and Mrs William Beauman, I, the wife
of the governor, had something to say, but I was finding
it hard to put into words. *Well, they must have looked
mighty foolish with that cannon,* I said at last, because
what I wanted to say seemed to have something to do
with the muscular straining of absurd whiskered men,
who had taken a brass cannon on the backs of horses so
they could have a proper battle. It was not that sort of
thing, this affray in the middle of the bush with men
armed with a few old flintlocks, but our husbands had
hoped for a bit of glory from it. *Oh,* Mrs Miles said, *we
could not have told them, though, could we? They would
never have listened.* Mrs Peeper made the teacup rattle
in its saucer, shrieking—I had wondered at times if Mrs
Peeper was not a trifle vulgar—*Listen to us, love, never!
And it was such a big cannon, and such a shiny one!* We
all laughed, and even Mrs Beauman cracked her face
enough to show a tooth or two, and then a silence came
over us all, that Mrs Miles had to break, by saying in a
way that sounded rather loud in the silence: *But you
know, I would love to have been able to go with them,
or just go.* Then she laughed her studied silly laugh, and
put a pretty little hand up in front of her mouth, as if
shocked at the words, and keeping in others like them.
We all laughed with her, but we all knew then what we
shared, and it was not an interest in mauves or pinks
or rosewater.

Huge hail suddenly began to fall into the dull afternoon,
and we could forget our tittering and teacups, and under
cover of the chaos of the hail we languid ladies could
act and exclaim. We rushed to the window so our silks
made a sighing draught, and rustled against the panes,

until Mrs Beauman suddenly cried out with such passion
that the words caught in her throat, so that she had to
stop and cough them clear and start again: *Oh, I want
to feel them against me!* Mrs Beauman of the plaster
perfection, Mrs Beauman of the practiced arch of eyebrow
was flushed, and her eyes, as a rule beautiful and languid,
were now grown small and tight, as if anxious or desperate. She had become humid and swollen, as if her
skin was too tight, watching the gigantic hail bounce on
the lawn in that mad way.

She saw me watching as we stood there by the window,
and met my eyes, and tried to laugh something like her
usual deft belittling laugh, and said, *Oh, hail, it brings
me out in a rash of passion, I must see it up close.*
Although she was too finely bred to lead the way out to
the verandah, she followed me so swiftly I felt pursued.

Out there I knew what she meant about a rash of
passion. The air was cool and electric and the sound of
the hail was like a crowd, the gigantic hailstones pouring
down out of the sky and bouncing on the grass like living
creatures. Already the lawn was grey with them and the
air was full of their low unlikely roaring. I felt an obscure
passion in my own chest, some longing for large action,
something to match this outlandish performance of the
heavens. I watched Mrs Beauman as she was drawn to
the edge of the verandah, where the air was full of spray
and the noise was something you wanted to join, and
we watched, Mrs Peeper and Mrs Miles and I, as Mrs
Beauman was drawn down the steps and out into the
tumult until she was standing on the lawn, not like any
languid wealthy wife now, but like someone mad, with
her hair already streaking dark down her cheeks. *Mrs
Beauman!* I heard Mrs Peeper exclaim beside me, but it
was not to call her back, but seemed rather as if she
were reminding herself that this woman, in her green silk

that was darkening in great streaks and blobs now, and
starting to cling to her thighs, was the same Mrs Beauman
we had known as the ornament of any drawing-room.
We watched the hail bouncing off the head and shoulders
of this other Mrs Beauman, watched her hold out her
hands so her cupped palms made the hail bounce, watched
her turn around under the blast from the sky, so that
we saw at one moment her face, pale and shining, and
the next moment saw her dark silken back. The Mrs
Beauman we knew, the Mrs Beauman of controlled laughs,
of satire that made smaller souls laugh so loudly it was
inelegant enough to raise the eyebrows of the servants:
Mrs Beauman who was never seen to move a muscle of
that perfect face except in the precise way she intended—
this was Mrs Beauman, standing like a monk, clothed in
concentration under a hail of hail.

I watched, and envied, and tried to make my feet
follow her down to the edge of the verandah, down the
steps, and out into that white noise, but I was afraid.
How could I have imagined myself in charge of platoons
of swarthy men, battlefields, prancing horses? I was not
brave enough even to risk the sniggering of a few silly
servants: I was afraid, fearful of a bit of frozen water
and what a few minions might think! There was a chill
that had nothing to do with the ice-filled air, but which
was my own vision of myself not making history at all,
but living out my life in pinks and mauves, hesitating
forever on the edge of verandahs.

When the hail thinned suddenly and stopped, there
was a silence which the three of us filled with laughing
and exclaiming and the vague cheery crowings that the
moment seemed to call for. Mrs Beauman was cheerful,
rueful, laughing too, for all the world as if she had merely
been out walking and been taken by surprise by the storm.
Oh! Oh! she kept crying, *Look at this, oh!* and shook out

the drenched green skirt in a futile way, fanning it against her legs so we could hear wet silk and wet petticoats against her flesh. *Hail is so WET!* she exclaimed, being girlish now and pretending dismay, but her eyes were shining and her mouth lascivious from her debauch. We all laughed and bustled, and servants were called to run baths, and bring dry clothes, and it was all a cosy domestic matter of an amusing mishap, not a passion unsuitable and shocking in a lady of plaster perfection.

I need not even tell you that we were not so crass as to point out that this was no accident, or to ask her how it felt to lift your palms to that torrent from a deafening heaven. But I had been made small, I had been exposed— to myself if to no one else—as being no heroic Joan, no maker of history, but simply Lady Stoneman, the somewhat insipid wife of one of the less spectacular governors of one of Her Majesty's dullest corners of Empire.

I was humbled as I watched Mrs Beauman still glowing from her passion. She was making history in her own way as I had to find a way to make my own, even though mine, I now saw, was unlikely to have anything to do with hot-eyed poets, or cavorting horses, or even the ecstasy of ice against fevered flesh. My destiny would be unremarkable, but I would have to embrace it just the same.

JOAN

I left Duncan not on a night of moon while stockmen snored and dreamed of wild exploits, but among quinces in syrup and bottled peas like pearls. Duncan and I had come to the Show to look at the cattle for professional reasons, and we had stayed for the sheepdogs, marvelling with everyone else while small men in hats clucked and whistled to their dogs and made them perform absurd feats with sheep. I found myself becoming anxious, watching so much obedience, such intelligence, packed into the parcel of a mere dog.

It was all new to me, and intriguing: those dogs, and the huge-uddered milkers rolling their gigantic eyes at us, and the enormous hairy tassels of bulls, and the small skilful men and women who moved quietly among them with shovels of dung and bales of hay. So by the time we reached the Agricultural Hall I was in a trance of strangeness, and after so many months seeing only the same few people day after day, I was as if hypnotized by such an extravagance of strange faces, such an excess of other people's eyes flickering across mine as we jostled past. So many souls, so many stories, were whipping me up to madness.

I paused in the crush before a display of bottled edibles: serrated carrots, diamonds of sliced pale beans, onions and purple cabbage and peas all packed like jewels in their gleaming jars, no longer food so much as a tribute to ingenuity.

I paused to wonder, and when I looked around I saw that Duncan had continued to move on, past the displays of pointless labor, and in a moment his tweed shoulders had disappeared behind a cluster of flowered hats. A few steps would have taken me back to him: he would have turned, taken my hand, made some small joke about losing me, might have suggested a pot of tea and scones in the refreshment tent. But those few simple steps did not occur to me. Without quite planning, without anything as deliberate as choice, moving by a kind of gravity, I found that I had stepped sideways, into a narrow tunnel that led to the back of a display of apples and pears, arranged so as to represent the main thoroughfares of Mudgee. It was the impulse of a moment, and the shuffle and buzz of the crowd was instantly muffled by a roof of fruit, the glare of lights was darkened and I was alone. I knew that if I did not make the choice of moving back out into the lights, I could remain alone here, and not be found.

Some decisions are over in the wink of an eye and others spin themselves out into a whole tale of their own. I had not made any decision yet, but when I found a fruit box to sit on in this dim sloping space, and discovered that when I sat on it I could see out through a chink in the display and watch the crowd, my action seemed more intentional: the act of sitting gave it a domesticity and permanence it had not had until then.

Duncan appeared in my line of sight after a moment: I watched him glance around, crane over heads, wave at someone he thought was me: I watched him shuffle and

turn on the spot, always sure I was somewhere behind
him, watched his face gradually close in on itself with
anxiety. At last he walked purposefully off, through with
many backward glances, and I guessed that he would
spend some time lurking around the powder room (but
first, blushing and cross, would have to ask where it was
and weather a suspicious stare from someone), and perhaps after that he would go to the tent where lost children
waited and wailed.

Trance had me in its grip, but not so much that I was
not cunning: I was not so entranced as to come out from
behind my peas and pears yet, for a calculating part of
me knew that Duncan would be back, and I continued
to crouch and peer, watching the country folk whose
world I was leaving behind.

A woman in a huge hat of a rather electric shade of
blue, that made her face corpse-like, stood pulling her
cardigan over her bust and stared, not at the display—
she looked a woman who had seen plenty of peas in
brine in her time—but at the crowd, at the sharp city
folk sniggering openly at so much innocent rustic en-
deavor, and marvelling, but with contempt, at the way
someone had spent days making sure no pea was out of
place.

Some good-hearted woman in an apron thriftily made
from an old cotton frock had worked hard and been
proud of what she had done, was perhaps even this same
woman, ill at ease in her electric-blue hat and the new
cardigan from Mark Foys that was, she now realized, a
little tight over the bust. She stared at the city folk and
watched them nudging each other and smirking, and I
crouched behind the jars and was a traitor to everything:
a traitor to Duncan, gone off in search of me while I
hid, a traitor to this kindly woman with her good heart,
(for I had sniggered, I had scorned!), and even a traitor

to the smart folk in their sharp shoddy clothes (no quality from Mark Foys for them, that would last for donkey's years, the look was the thing for them, not how a thing would last), and I despised them and feared myself for all that I was, and for what I was allowing myself to do. This was the world I had been living in with Duncan, the life of scones, the life where preserved quinces mattered, the life where women did not care if they got fat, and red-faced, and elephantine of ankle, as long as their scones were crumbly and as long as their marmalade could bear the test of being held up to the light by women who knew cloudy marmalade when they saw it, and who did not mind giving you a piece or two of advice on such matters.

Just look at that arrangement, I heard a woman say in a voice like church, *who'd have thought it possible,* and the man with her, in a hat and a blue-striped suit, guffawed in a way that said he was not going to be intimidated by any number of peas in brine, and said *Blooming waste of blooming time, I'd as soon eat them and be done with it.*

I was right in knowing that Duncan would be back: there he was again among the cardigans and the flat country hats, and now I was seized with a terrible stifling excitement and a deadly glee, and watching him this time I felt my trance lifting: I had taken those few steps in a cowardly stupor, but now I could pretend the decision was irrevocable: now I could agree with what my feet had already said, that I had abandoned my husband.

I watched and crouched, breathless with the farcical enormity of what I was doing, and I wondered if he knew, as I did, that he was listening to his watch tick out the first few minutes of the birth of the new Duncan, the Duncan who had been abandoned at the Show, in the Agricultural Hall, by his reckless wife. He stood among the shifting tides of people enjoying their day out, and I watched him become angry, kicking hard at the sawdust on the ground and ramming his hands into the pockets of his tweed so hard I thought his fists might burst right through.

Anger faded quickly in Duncan, though: he was not a man to keep up a good head of rage for long. I saw him become anxious then, biting those freckled lips of his and shifting from one foot to the other, whirling around as if he had heard me call him, peering and straining through all the people. I watched him rub his eyes where they were weary with willing me to appear, smiling and apologetic, from behind a large man with a pipe, or a clutch of women with flowered frocks. I watched him take off his hat and inspect inside it, running his hand around the brim as if I might be hiding there, saw him look at his watch, then take it off, slowly, being careful with that worn and slippery leather strap that I knew so well. He wound it slowly, carefully, held it to his ear, and looked solemn, listening to it tick.

There were moments when I could see he had convinced himself I was playing a joke on him, and I crouched lower in shame, seeing his face serene and even amused, such a man that even after hours of standing waiting he was prepared to forgive me my little joke. A joke would have been cruel enough, but his face never showed that he could conceive of cruelty worse than that.

The afternoon wore on, my fruit box became hard, and I watched Duncan grow pale, insubstantial with the doubts and fears that I could see filling him now. I grew hungry among so much massed nutrition, and when Duncan had wandered away a few steps I snaked out my hand into the display and took a pear and an apple. They were hard as rocks, both of them, since they had to keep for all the time the Show would last—it would never do for the display to turn brown and putrid, or for the slick city folk to snigger about clouds of flies around the map of the main thoroughfares of Mudgee done in seven kinds of pear and eleven kinds of apple. So I ate my bitter fruit, and burped on its hardness, and pondered my own hardness of heart, that I could sit for a whole endless afternoon watching my husband grow wan and worn, haggard with waiting, bloodless with a growing fear that he would not confess to himself.

At last the crowds thinned, bells began to peal, and people in white coats began to herd everyone towards the doors. But Duncan would not be herded. He stood immovable in his thick brown shoes while the men in white gestured at him: he stood, I could see his mouth, a little stiff now and livid with the long hours of patience, saying the same thing over and over, and he would not move: not until one of the men in white, a large red-nosed one who looked impatient to get home to where his wife would have his tea ready for him on the stove, laid a large hand on Duncan's arm.

Then I watched in astonishment at what I had already done to my mild Duncan, for he wheeled on the red-nosed man with rage, took aim at his nose, and let fly with one fist, then the other, and sent one of those brown shoes too, into the poor shins of that red-nosed man. I saw then that, if I had been crouching on my box, watching and waiting for the possibility that I might change my mind, it was too late now: Duncan was no longer the peaceful man who had woken up beside me that morning. I saw, in the expressions of outrage and righteous sternness on the faces of the white-coated men (hired for just such an emergency, but who would ever have imagined it would take the violent efforts of three large men to remove a spectator from the excitements of the Agricultural Hall?) that Duncan was no longer a peaceful man. I had fractured his peace for ever, and I sat shivering with awe at my power.

Joan Makes History

SCENE EIGHT

In the 1870s Australians prided themselves that
trains would truly open this country where only
kangaroos had hopped or Cobb's horse-drawn
coaches rattled through. I, Joan, was an
adventurous woman this time and set out to
sample as many modes of transport as the country
could offer.

I was off then, away on the open road with the small shammy bag containing William's wizened gold nuggets: off into my own future. No more crouching red-faced over the fire, poking at corned beef in the pot, no more lugging water up from the creek, and no more of William's caresses under the fly net at night: no more of hearing his voice crack and go hoarse, ragged with lust, or what he called love: no more feeling his eyes on me every minute, even in our bed, where I could not escape his soft looks, for they were caught in the mirror he angled to inflame himself, watching how he penetrated my dark flesh, and how it arched and bucked under him.

And where was I going? It was enough for me that I had begun my journey, and the journey was the simpler for there being but two roads out of this place: I could head west, or I could head east. I had no answers to any such questions, except the answer of movement, by which one forgot most things. *On!* the inner voice commanded, and on I went, turning my back on the past like every other coward, for surely I was a coward to steal away with William's gold.

Walkabout was something they accused us all of, and used it as the pretext for letting us scour, and scrub, and

lug, and display our charms to them in the thickets of
their bedclothes, and for giving us nothing of substance.
Even my William, who was better than most, had only
guffawed when I had revealed to him that I was a woman
of destiny: *Oh,* he had laughed, *what need have you of
destiny, when mine is at your disposal?* He had curled
my fingers around his warm worm of destiny then, no
more than amused at my flight of fancy.

But it was no blackfeller compulsion that set me on
the road away from William: it was good sound sense,
such as the clay-colored folk thought they had a monopoly
of. I had *plenty tucker, plenty mutton,* as William was
fond of reminding me in a threatening way when I wearied
of his blandishments, and it was true he had bought me
plenty fine frock-frocks from the catalogue. But of such
trifles a life was not being made. I had other ambitions
for myself than being the dusky paramour of lascivious
William.

Here I was, then, with nothing much but William's
nuggets making a single suggestive bump in my bodice
where nature had provided me with none, and in my
bundle a pair of woolen stockings, a shawl, my piece of
false hair, and one or two other useful items. Like every
other roaming adventurer, I stood looking up and down
the road, waiting for the next thing to declare itself to
me.

Feet were my first friends. Mine were well shod, in a
pair of well-fitting boots that William had had made for
me, and which he had polished himself of an evening
by the fire until they gleamed along every wrinkle. I
strode out along the streets, heading east and hopefully,
but the buildings passed too slowly, too many men stared
rudely into my face, and I had a sense of trudging and
getting nowhere, of stifling down there among others
afoot, and of being too vulnerable to apprehension and

all the indignant shouting and nugget-brandishing that would tiresomely result.

So I hopped astride a bicycle as it leaned against a lamp post, and wobbled off down the street. I had not had enough practice at this bicycle business, just a few giggling goes on William's big black Swallow, but I had never been able to make it *Skim The Road* as its advertisement claimed, and the sight of me astride it had always reminded William of me astride other kinds of machines, fleshier ones, and he had tipped me off, and into the hut, and onto the bed, before I had properly mastered this device. But I sprang on this one and made all the haste I could around the first corner. I loved the feel of air rushing past my face, and I was hot with the desire to be on my way, anywhere, quickly.

But that saddle did not fit me, perhaps because it was made for a person with protuberances where I had none, and this Swallow was much too big for me, so that after only a short time I began to pant, and ache, and strain and sweat over the gleaming handlebars, and knew that other gentlemen on other Swallows would be *Skimming The Road* after me at a speed greater than I could manage. I could imagine their indignation, their congested and frustrated ire, that would have liked to hit me, but had to be held in check because I was a female, and a darky, so that it had to be compressed into angry gestures and threatening shouts: I could imagine the way their faces would swell around their moustaches and their voices grow hoarse: oh, I could too easily imagine it, and it filled me with weariness.

So I left the Swallow, propped against a convenient fence, and tried to walk away as if I had nothing to do with it, but also with a good turn of speed. I was able to round a corner and watch from behind an oleander as five gentlemen in plus fours rode by, saw, shouted, rode back, dismounted, and stood for a long time gesturing and peering and smoothing with their hands the leather of the saddle, and exclaiming at each other before they finally got back on their bicycles, and the one on his penny-farthing leapt up onto it above them all, and wobbled dangerously before picking up speed. Two of them pedalled slowly behind the rest, wheeling the stolen one between them shamefaced like a miscreant.

But the urge was on me now to cover much ground, and to place myself and the bump in my bodice beyond the reach of anyone who might think they had a right to them. So I stepped out quickly and became cunning, leaving the road behind and finding my way up hillsides of trees, along gullies of ferns, and having not forgotten how to creep up on a goanna and bake it in its skin over a few coals, I did not go hungry. And what a pleasure it was, baked goanna taken in solitude! I sang to myself as I wandered on, led by a dragonfly darting ahead of me through the trees, or following the warblings of currawongs at dawn, or kookaburras at dusk, or wallaby tracks in the dust until I had to make them up.

A track, then a road, then a town, gave themselves up to me at last, and I put my boots back on (I could not catch goannas in boots, I could not even seem to eat them in boots), and my frock-frock (also removed, the better for listening to dragonflies), and descended on civilized man.

In my frock-frock and my boots, and with my straight hair and light-brown skin from my unknown father (his skin was speckled like an old leaf with freckles, and she thought his name was Charlie, it was all Mum could ever tell me, and she did not care much), I was a person of some presence, although unmistakably a blackfeller. So I held my head up while I bought another stretch of journey with one of William's bits of dirt, and took my place in the train. *To the Junction?* they asked, and I said *Yes.* I was not interested to know what *Junction:* to know this was a train bound for the *Junction* was plenty of knowledge for me.

A train! I speak of it now casually, as though stepping on trains came naturally, as if I had done it a thousand times before, or even once before. But, I will tell you as being between friends, this was the first train I had ever boarded, and in fact the first train I had ever seen. I had heard about them from William, and from Violet down the road, who had gone on a train once to find her Douglas in the city and lure him back: but this was my first actual train.

I knew that blackfellers on a train did not excite too much curiosity, for Violet was another white boss's gin like myself, and had travelled without causing a stir. I wished to avoid the curiosity of others, and knew that if I truly had a cautious white man's blood flowing in my veins, I would not risk a train, but would stick to feet on dirt. But my own curiosity was too great: I could not resist.

I had heard from Violet how you bought a bit of paper from a man in a cage, and sat on a wooden seat, and how there was a dunny that you could see the ground out the bottom of, that you were not supposed to use when the train was in a station. All this I found to be true, and more besides: Violet had done her best to make a train noise, and we had laughed so loudly that William had come in to see what all the noise was about, and he had laughed too, when he heard Violet's train noise and saw her eyes roll, describing the blasts of smoke from the engine and the great speed of the train's progress. *It left me stomach behind when it started,* Violet claimed, *and it was two days later it caught up with me.*

Now I knew what she meant, and I was afraid of the way the trees and stones moved past the window, all blurred and dizzy, and of the thunderous clacking and rattling of the box we sat in. But there was a nice chatty stickybeak busybody of a knitting woman in the box with me, an old grey-haired auntie sort of person, Mrs Cheeseman from Brewarrina. She agreed that she was a long way from home, and after treating me to all the reasons, she began to probe my own recent past and how it was that I found myself, *a nice native girl like yourself,* as she called me, on this train going to *the Junction.* Mrs Cheeseman had a way of not listening, and of interrupting you to ask *Where exactly is your home, dearie?* and *After the Junction, dearie, where exactly do you go from there?* and other questions I did not wish to have to answer. Nice native girls like myself can always feign stupidity, so I did for Mrs Cheeseman: *Oh, such a lovely home, Mrs Blenkinsop is ever so kind,* I gushed, *Oh it was so hot out that place, Mrs Cheeseman, well, Mrs Blenkinsop she fainted dead away every afternoon at three o'clock, Mr Blenkinsop he had to give her medicine from the brown bottle.*

Well, Mrs Cheeseman was no fool, she knew something was awry, and began to eye the bump in my bodice, so that when the train slowed and clashed into a town, I whisked up my bundle from the floor and said *Bye-bye Mrs Cheeseman, I hope your niece be better soon,* and made ready to get off. But she held me by the arm, saying, *No dear, this is not the Junction yet dearie, you must not get off here,* and Mrs Cheeseman's grip was strong, and I saw the way she was looking around for a man in a uniform to question me and delve into the secrets of my bodice, so I brought cunning to bear on the situation. *Okay Mrs Cheeseman,* I said and sat down grinning my amiable blackfeller grin, but when the whistle

blew and the train began to move, I was up quick as a
flash, grabbed the bundle, and shot out the door and off
the train before Mrs Cheeseman could so much as stand
up: so it was that I found myself on all fours, panting,
with a grazed hand and gravel in one knee, my bonnet
askew and everyone staring, on the platform at some
place that was not *the Junction*.

I picked myself up with a great show of rue, and, as
if I had been on the run all my life, I threw more dust
in the eyes of any pursuers by asking the way to the
Catholic school (it was a town big enough, in my cunning
I was sure there would be one). But I had been too smart
this time for my own good. *My word yes*, said a man
on a buggy who had watched me pick myself up. *You
mean the Native Welfare, I am going past there myself,
jump up behind now*. This was not what I had intended:
I had intended listening solemnly to long explanations
of *left* and *right* and *you can't miss it*, and once out of
the station I intended to take every *right* where they had
said *left*, every *left* where they had said *right*, and to
succeed in missing it. But here was destiny suggesting
another plan, and I surrendered for the moment.

You are older than the general run of them, this man
observed when he had got the horse going. *They like to
get them young and train them up*. I nodded and made
my eyes go somewhat poppy and my mouth slack-lipped:
I watched him like this until he grew uneasy under my
idiot stare, and said no more until we arrived. *Here you
are, lass*, he said loudly and clearly, *I hope they can make
a useful Godfearing domestic out of you*, although his
look said clearly that he did not think it possible.

I knew about the Native Welfare, of course, and had
promised myself never to have a child, so I need never
know the anguish of having it taken from my arms and
sent to the Native Welfare people. I did not intend to

167

delay in the vicinity of any such place, but I was obliged to hover by the gate until the man's snail-like buggy was out of sight: I hovered and pretended to be having trouble with a bootlace, hanging for balance onto the gate that struck chill into my hand.

But before the obliging man and his horse had moved out of sight, the great door of the building opened and I had to step aside for a long column of children. The brown serge they wore made their dark skins sallow, and there was a dullness of eye to them all, a droop of shoulder. These children did not look around as they walked, but trudged along in pairs looking at the ground as if their futures were written there.

They were children who had been numbed: they looked as though they did not care any more. With them from the interior of the dark building came a stream of air smelling of carbolic and furniture polish, and of too many humans too close together and not happy.

There was a line of black boys, then one of black girls, and beside them walked their white guardians: a long thin melancholy man of feeble whiskers and jutting chin, a man himself as beaten and glazed as these children, and two women, one so stout she seemed to pant in her flesh, and roll from one foot to the other, and the other a pointy-faced plain woman, plainer even than myself, with ears far too large for her head, and too much on display, the way her thin hair was pulled back over her skull.

As I watched, one of the girls suddenly burst out of her ranks and before the fat woman could move, or the large-eared one catch her, she had shoved her way into the lines of boys, and was clinging to one of the grey-faced boys, who clung back, both in a terrible silence, while the thin man, the fat woman, and the one with ears were parting the rows of boys to reach them and

168

drag them apart. They were silent throughout: silent while they were being pulled away from each other, silent while the girl was marched back to her place, silent while the boys' lines were made straight again. Then the lines of children went on trudging out the gate as if nothing had happened and I watched the face of the girl as she passed me: her small face was without expression, not even a look of hopelessness. This was all she could expect from this bit of her life: to touch the skin of her brother for a few moments once a day.

It was hard to imagine happy futures for any of these children, removed from their mother's humpies—for their own good, naturally—and trained up to be useful. As a person of mixed blood myself, I might have suffered the same fate if such an ingenious scheme had been devised a few years earlier, and I could not get away fast enough from this place: the very air threatened me with its miasma of lost souls. *On!* I cried to myself, and made for the open road.

My next conveyance was a coach, boarded on an impulse as it changed its horses at an inn on the edge of town. *Where to, then?* the driver rudely asked, when I approached him, and I mumbled *The coast, mister,* at hazard, and he nodded in an exasperated sort of way.

What coast? Not knowing where I was, I had no idea, but knew that one road out of town must lead eventually to some coast, somewhere or other, for I knew my nation was an island: and it gave an appearance of knowing where you wanted to go, to say something definite like *To the coast.*

As a coach going to the coast ought to do, this one stank of fish, and was tightly packed with travellers. It was a mad extravagance to be in a coach. But I was still afeared by what I had seen at the Native Welfare, and wished to make haste away. Besides, I had never before

169

been rich with nuggets, and probably never would be
again, so I relished the plush seat of the coach and the
way the bush went past at a good speed, and the way
the other passengers and myself passed the time of day
with each other.

The other female in this coach was a Miss Haines, a
very tightly curled and corseted rouged lady with a way
of saying *if you don't mind,* such as: *Give me a nice leg
of mutton any day, none of your foreign muck if you
don't mind,* or: *Oh no, I was not obliged to come out to
the colony, I had a very nice position in Giddingly if you
don't mind.*

I did start to mind in the end, for Miss Haines was
tiresome with her fine mincing ways and tiny tight mouth,
and the way she made sure no part of her person came
in contact with any part of the person of the black girl
beside her, and when she was persuaded to reveal that
she was going to a place called Eden, the hairy-nostrilled
man Barnaby exclaimed, *Oh, the new barmaid then are
you, love?* and Miss Haines flushed and said, *Do you
mind,* and became highly interested in the view from the
window.

Barnaby did not mind us knowing all his secrets, for
he was a coarse guffawing sort of man, who was forever
nudging Herman next to him, an acquaintance of sorts,
it seemed, but Herman did not conceal how wearisome
he found this nudging Barnaby. Then there was a huge
pale man with cropped yellow hair and ears like feet
sticking out of his head: his name was something that
sounded as if he was about to bring up his breakfast,
and his enormous hands, each one the size of a dinner
plate, were as bright red as if they had been boiled.
Barnaby, not one to be backward in asking questions of
a personal nature, shouted at him to ask why they were
that color, and we all craned to look at them, resting

huge and glowing on his powerful thighs. Barnaby poked
and bellowed: *Red, red, why red? Looky here, mine white,
see, white-white, you red-red,* and it was easy to see that
this fair foreign man knew what was being asked, that
he was sick of being asked, and that he could not think
of how to explain without the necessary words of English.
We all watched, even lemon-lipped Miss Haines, as the
huge man demonstrated cold, shivering and hugging himself, shaking the fingers of his big raw hands, until suddenly Mr Jellicoe, who was going to join the bank at
Eden, exclaimed, *Frostbite! If they do not fall off altogether, they turn red, I have heard.* This was more than
Mr Jellicoe had previously said all at once, and like the
big man's hands he turned scarlet and subsided in his
seat, and now that the mystery was solved, the red-handed
man was no longer of much interest.

Through all this I was the grinning darky, feigning
being too shy to do more than giggle and cover my mouth
with my hand, as that was the easiest way to avoid more
stickybeaking and the best way to enjoy the spectacle of
people behaving.

We had all gone a bit silent after the red-handed man
had been explained, and at that moment the road took
a sudden turn downwards as if at a line drawn through
the bush. We hung onto the benches under us that threatened to tip us all head over turkey: the jolting became
so extreme we could hardly hold on, and I could see
nothing but the bush all crooked out the window of the
coach. Then it was decided that we must all dismount,
for the brake was smoking against the wheel and the
horses, poor creatures, were tossing their heads and slipping and sliding on the dirt.

I thought at first there must be a tribe in the bush,
hidden among the trees and green ferns in all these
mysterious clefts and folds of valley: for when the coach

171

had been left behind a little way, and we were all on foot straggling down this yellow road, I could hear things calling to each other: clear, soft metal sounds like chimes with a human voice.

Barnaby caught up to me and saw me listening: whiskery Barnaby had taken a fancy, I could tell. *Bellbirds,* Barnaby said, *funny kind of racket they make.* And, embracing me so suddenly he knocked the air clean out of my chest, he went on talking while he propelled me off the road and behind a tree. *Oh, you hot slut!* he exclaimed. Behind that watching tree, with Barnaby pressing the flesh of his mouth against various parts of my person, I found him repugnant, his whiskers coarse, his hands ungentle, his clothes odorous and repellent. *Go 'way, go 'way,* I shrilled at him, and scratched at the hands holding me until they let me go and oh, the bewilderment, the what-have-I-done, the indignation and the surprise of this fishy dolt, to be spurned!

He still did not believe me, in spite of the graze of blood on the back of his hand, and showed his teeth, saying, *Oh you black firebrand you, you are a tease, you want it too, upon my word you do.* We struggled in an undignified way among the dead leaves, and only when the toe of my boot struck Barnaby with enough force to make him stagger did he believe me.

This Eden seemed as far off as the other one, and the coach was oppressive when we got back inside with Barnaby glowering and muttering, and with Miss Haines refusing even to sit alongside of me now, and with Herman smelling powerfully of his pipe, although he had put it away back in his pocket when we had remounted. We had all gone quiet now, except that Barnaby said from time to time, jerking a thumb at various landmarks, *Not long now, not long now.* He could hardly wait for Eden, and nor could I.

It was Herman, next to me now, who broke the silence that was starting to stifle us, and enquired where I was bound. This time I was prepared, and had a long garbled giggling story prepared, of how I was *looking for me auntie, by the name of Auntie Bess, me Mum died see and she says, you gotta find your auntie,* and so on. It was easy to run on and watch their smiles grow weary finally, and I finished it off by saying loudly, *Might getta job, I learned how to clean real good, up Mrs Oliphant's place.*

Herman did not appear to be altogether fooled by my performance, and watched me with a shrewdness that made me uneasy until I realized he was enjoying it as much as I was. He was a Yankee, perhaps that was the difference: he was a large bristling man, black of beard and cross of brow, and seemed to know a thing or two about most things, not just about the whaling that was his profession.

And it was Herman who, when we reached *the coast,* persuaded me to join him in boarding a small boat that would take us to another part of the coast where he had business to conduct. I felt it only right that I should sample a short sea voyage, so I stepped on board behind Herman with my bundle of things, and prepared to enjoy being something of an old salt.

But this was a small creaking wallowing sort of boat, and I was not accustomed to any manner of boat, and felt uneasy of stomach at the way it heaved up and down in the troughs of the sea and jerked me around as I sat on a slippery bench and tried to fix my mind on something that did not move, and tried harder still not to think of and certainly, after the first indelible glance, not to look at the water slopping around our feet in the bottom of the boat, greenish water in which several decaying fish heads floated, and a long thread of the innards of something with a morsel of liver attached, that stretched and contracted with each toss of the boat.

The less I thought about these details, the more uncertain my own innards felt about the whole enterprise and the more green I felt myself going as the waves crashed over the front of the boat. It no longer seemed to matter that I was travelling, and it was hard to remember exactly what it was I was travelling to, or from. With an effort I could recall William and dreadful Barnaby and could remember various bicycles, streets, trees—my mind moved fast, trying to fill itself with clean dry images—but in the end everything went a sort of grey shot with stars before my eyes, and for a while I felt nothing but my insides turning out and the cold wet wood of the gunwale I clung to, leaning out over the cold green waves.

So much for boats, then: they were no way to travel. When I stepped off the boat and felt a solid jetty under my trembling legs I swore I would never again go on water, that I was a terrestrial creature, and that man, and perhaps more particularly woman, was not meant to venture on that cold unfriendly medium, and would have been equipped with gills if that had been intended.

There was a man waiting at the dock with a wagon and a big square horse that would take us up the hill to the township, and I got up beside Herman in the wagon, and calmed my fluttering stomach and my tingling fingers and toes by watching the calm dignified buttocks of this humble brown horse and telling over to myself like beads on a rosary all his paraphernalia: bit and bridle, collar and hames, saddle and girths, shaft-leathers and crupperstraps, until I was soothed, and could again enjoy my journey and my companion.

Herman proved a teller of tall tales after my own heart. Sitting on a bollard down on the pier—as close as I would

go to the water—he told me of the whales he had seen
harpooned, the arms and legs he had seen snapped and
crunched in tangles of ropes or between gunwales or in
the gripe of monstrous agonized fish leaving trails of gore
in the water. He had a fine way with words, this Yankee,
though his tales tended towards infinite elaboration of
insignificant detail, and frankly I was sure that most of
them were extravagant invention. But he sat in a gentle
way on the bollard, drawing these ferocious pictures before
my eyes, looking off into the bay as if the words were
written there for him to read off.

His tales led to a certain fondness, and to certain
fondlings to which I found I was not averse. *You are the
Eve of my Eden,* Herman told me, and I enjoyed his
hyperbole, and the way I could make him rumble with
laughter at a few tall tales of my own. I told him the
history of William, who had taken me so young and silly
that I had been flattered, and fearful of my orphaned
outcast future, and with Herman I did not bother to be
half-witted, but told my tales with all the gift of the gab
at my command.

I enjoyed Herman, but my life did not belong with
him: it was not for Herman that I had taken to the road.
So, before too much fondness grew between our skins, I
went down to meet him on our pier with the open road
on my mind once again. Herman was sitting on his bollard
smoking as if it took all his attention, and did not turn
to me when I sat on the next bollard. There lying blame-
lessly at anchor out in the bay was the *Chesapeake,* which
would shortly take Herman back onto the sea, and he
would watch seagulls and harpoons fly and smell the
stench of blubber rendering. Perhaps he would himself
be carried to the depths of the ocean, tangled up with
some maddened whale with an iron spear in it and a
few miles of wild rope streaming after. Perhaps in another

port another girl would hear his tales, light his pipe for him, admire his bristling hairs and his soft way with a few words, and on other bollards he would stare out at the horizon with the smoke blue around his head, preparing to say farewell.

I am going on, I said. *I am off, Herman,* I said, and was pleased at the surprise on his face, and the way he drew me between his knees as he sat on his bollard, and placed his large hands around my waist: *Well,* he said, *There are not two like you in this wide world, of a surety.* We parted, then, with the soft hankering glances on his side, not mine, and I set off again for my unknown future.

I had had an adventure or two since I had taken the two steps across William's kitchen and out the door. I had covered many miles by different devices: I had become an expert on the subject of transport, and now I had the feeling that I was on the last leg of my voyage. Certainly there was no persistence by which William could possibly trace my checkered journey.

I sat behind the rising and falling haunches of a horse pulling a wagon full of whalebone bound for the torsos of the ladies of Sydney, beside a hard-breathing man with long white hairs springing out of his nostrils. When, after some miles, he had tired of flicking at the flies on the horse's rump with the reins and turned to me to make a little conversation, I was ready for him. In his slow way he asked me where I was bound, and I had an answer: *Sydney,* I told him. *I am on my way to Sydney, I am a bareback rider by profession, and the circus is in my blood.* The words seemed strange, out here on this peaceful dappled track with leaves all around us, and a fine fragrance of eucalyptus making everything sweet and simple, but it was a satisfaction to have such an answer, and I enjoyed the way this whiskery old gent craned round to have a good look at me, and see what a bareback rider with the circus in her blood might look like. *I have always been a performer,* I told him, warming to the truth of the words: *performance has been my whole life.* I could see I was impressing this simple soul, and that he knew the truth when he heard it, and I sat more eagerly now, staring forward past the huge haunches of the horse, looking forward to my new life.

JOAN

I woke up at nights listening to my heart beating. It was anxious, even if I was not: it knew enough to know it would not beat forever, that each beat was one less from its quota, from my life. I lay counting and making vague funnelling plans that ended in deltas of possibilities, morasses of variables.

When they talked about me, what would they say I had made of my life? *Everything ahead of her,* the hypocritical ones might agree, and shake their heads. I, too, shook my head and even on occasion moaned to smother the sound of my impatient heart, too busy ticking my life away for my liking. *That Joan,* I heard them say, and wanted them to say it with a laugh, or admiration, or awe. *Ah, that Joan!* Perhaps then they would be proud of having known me in my early, green-haired phases, when they had not wanted to be seen with me. *But I must make history,* I had to remind myself, and sat up against the close darkness of the little room where I lay alone, stifled by the thudding of the tireless machine in my chest. There were nights when I listened and waited for it to slow, give a last few flickering beats, and stop. Then I would be freed from the heavy weight of destiny that lay upon me.

I was the only one now watching my destiny. I was hidden like a seed buried in its furrow: Duncan could not have found me, since I did not wish to be found, and had taken so many zigzagged turnings and back-trackings in my journey away from him in the Agricultural Hall. No, I was on my own now, every bond snapped. It was just me, Joan, alone with my glorious future.

I made history in a teashop for a while, where no one knew I was Joan who was making history, but where I was just Joan who was a bit on the slow side and inclined to forget which table had wanted the scones. How I loathed myself, walking between the tables, asking in a voice still trying to be dainty, although becoming more desperate as the minutes passed with the scones becoming harder: *What party was it ordered the scones?*

There was an Elsie there who guessed at sad and sentimental pasts for me: *Oh men, they are not to be trusted, are they love?* Elsie would hint as we cut crusts off bread together, and I would agree, but give her no further satisfaction, and her lips would go thin as she pressed the bread hard, gouging with her knife until she would think of another approach, and say with a sigh and a histrionic hand in the small of her back: *Little joys the kiddies are, but they break your heart as well, don't they, Joan?* Again I would agree, whipping my knife through the scone dough in the way I was learning, but giving her nothing more, just *Oh, my word yes,* and if I was feeling in a teasing mood a sigh or two that might speak volumes, or might not. Elsie's lips would go thin again, and I would watch her thinking behind her eyes, and she would shrug at last at the French toast she was arranging, and I could imagine her arranging the words for her Alf at home. He was a man who liked a good crisp sausage, she often confided, with a spud or two: *Alf, there is some sad story there,* I could imagine her saying, *but of course I am not one to pry, as you know, Alf.*

I thought of joining the circus when it came through and I went and gasped with the rest as the unlikely looking woman in spangles grinned a terrible weary grin at us while hanging by her ankle from a strap. But I could not remember that any history had ever been made in a circus.

Did I have to return to the fold of the family, back to bald Father and gold-toothed Mother, and live from the generosity of that bald man? But of course I could stand for Parliament. My tireless imagination ignited at the thought: *Me, Joan, a Member of Parliament,* and in the end, of course, when the silver was streaking through my hair in a distinguished and trustworthy way, I would be Prime Minister. On the day of my ordination or whatever it was that happened to Prime Ministers, the hairless man in the front row would embarrass everyone mightily by allowing shining tears to run down his face, and might even exclaim aloud in some barbaric tongue at the moment of investiture, so that the red-frocked beadles, or whoever they were, would exchange glances, wondering if the baldy was some sort of reffo ratbag who had sneaked in past the guards and would now have to be removed, preferably without making physical contact with his no doubt garlic-smelling person.

But the thought of returning to the fold of my family brought on a great weariness. I could not give up *all* hope of a future. *Dear Mother and Father,* I wrote at last, and travelled miles to post in a part of the city I never normally went. *I am well and happy. I am following my prospects for a while and do not wish to be found just now, but I will let you know from time to time how I am getting on. Your loving daughter, Joan:* except that when I first wrote this letter, in a moment of abstraction

I wrote *Your laughing daughter Joan,* and had to write it out again.

Because, you see, I could not face the tiresome questions, the endless planning and debating, the recriminations, the puzzlement, the demands to know what would happen next. I did not know what would happen next, and did not wish to have to answer any such questions.

Then, on a day of small fluffy clouds and a frivolous breeze in the trees of the park, my destiny was unfolded to me. A small striped lizard stopped in a crevice of bark, and I saw the flickering pulse beat in its neck and its tiny eye watching me. To this meek and watchful striped small lizard I announced on that golden morning: *I will be a man.*

A smug duck quacked at me but I was not deterred. *Jack,* I said in a forthright way, and thrust out my hand. *The name's Jack.* The lizard gulped and vanished around the corner of the trunk and a few leaves applauded overhead with a dry respectful sound. It was done, I was Jack, a woman of destiny.

Pants altered my heart. The soul of Joan had always been above the frivolous distinctions of sex, as my domed father had known when he had provided me with encyclopedias and sets of black pens: all the same, pants changed everything. I stood for hours in front of the mirror in my room, turning this way and that to snare every facet of Joan in pants and hair cut short with nail scissors.

If a man panics, he drowns. That was the first lesson I learned in my pants. I boarded the tram with a flourish, enjoying my pants and being able to be graceless, and flung myself onto the wooden slats of the seat the way I had spent a lifetime watching men do. I made the bench shake, as they did, and I sat with my knees wide apart, addressing my serge crotch to the woman opposite in the way that I, as a pathetic flimsy bit of woman, had so often been addressed by the crotches of confident men.

By the time the conductress came around with her gaping bag of coppers I was making bold with my eyes at this woman and she was responding with a shiftiness of eye, a tucking and retucking of ankles under her, and her hands were gripping the handle of her shopping basket so tightly I could watch the blood blocked in her knuckles. Such pleasure I felt at her awkwardness! I could barely contain a laugh of joy: the joy of power, of which I had known so little until now. In this case the power was hardly satisfying, being achieved with so little struggle, and all I could feel was scorn for this flustered woman, gripping her basket as if to strangle it, and I knew now how all silly creatures in skirts and blushes were of no account to the creatures in the pants, who had the power.

Suddenly, though, another kind of woman was upon me, flinty of eye and parrotlike of voice as she stood with her soiled palm stretched towards me saying *Fares please* in a challenging sort of way. In my pleasure at sitting spreadeagled on the bench and hounding, in a beginner's small way, that woman opposite, I had forgotten about such details as the fare, and was thrown into the kind of fluster that I can only describe, with shame, as female.

Ah! I heard myself exclaim. *Oh! So sorry,* I piped in an ingratiating way that made me cringe, and I fumbled and struggled with those pants, my enemy now, for I could not remember what I had done with my necessaries: without my woman's handbag I was thrown into womanly confusion, and tried to dig into the pockets of those pants, and explored the pockets of the jacket, and at last came upon my purse: a shameful and womanly affair I had not yet had time or thought to replace. I pulled it out of a pocket and felt those flinty eyes stripping soul from flesh as this woman saw through me. Women, I saw, were the weakest beings when they came in the form of blushing persons with shopping bags, but the strongest when they stood swaying confidently with the lurching of a tram, their lips grown thin, their eyes horribly knowing. *There we are, sorry, thank you, yes, thanks very much,* I heard myself hatefully gushing as I handed over my sweaty coppers, and saw the contempt in her eyes, and felt myself blushing like an idiot girl at my placating puny words so that even the woman opposite, I saw out of the corner of my fevered eye, was craning round the conductress now to get a good look at me, for she too had seen and heard that this bold crotch-displaying man opposite was all wrong.

I paid my coppers and left the tram at the next stop, stepped down and stood shakily in the gutter waiting for the panic of shame and fear to pass. A car roared close to me so I stepped back, stumbled, nearly fell under its wheels, felt myself splaying, scrabbling at the gutter to save myself, heard a man yell out of the car at me, *Wake up to yourself, mate.* I sat on a bench designed for the restoration of quivery old ladies, not brash young men in new suits: I sat there for a long time, watching the trams rumble by, considering to what extent pants do not a man make.

I stayed long enough in Sydney to make the worst of my mistakes there, and I promised myself to leave it when I had made every kind of fool of myself a man could. It was a place to learn a few tricks and to equip myself in the right ways so that I would have nothing, not a single handkerchief or turn of head, to shame me again.

At last, leaving mistakes behind like broken plates, I stepped on a train and went to marvellous Melbourne, where I could walk through streets even more confidently,

knowing that here I would never pass a certain bald man
in the street, frowning still for the loss of his daughter,
frowning at the skinny young man in the blue suit, cross
at him as at everyone for not being the apple of his
brown eye, his daughter who had vanished.

The bit of history I chose to make as a man was
humble, but in my pants I was making history by doing
nothing more thrilling than simply existing. In Melbourne
I was Jack, and everyone tipped Jack, the friendliest of
the waiters at the hot chophouse called the Galaxy, perhaps because of the extensiveness of its collection of
odors, out the back where the fat was poured into drums
and the patrons pissed. The Galaxy knew nothing of the
secret life of Jack, which was spent not in the arms of
any woman, nor—as the bolder patrons assumed because
of Jack's delicacy of figure and manner—in the arms of
any furtive man-loving man, either. Jack spent her spare
time walking the streets, never tiring of the way she could
boldly meet the eye of anyone, man or woman, that she
cared to: walking the streets and watching the trams,
being idle, unashamed, and bold in public in a way poor
Joan, for all her bluster, had never been.

At last, though, the joy wore off. I could meet any eye
I chose, and had met thousands of strangers' eyes now,
and was the richer for the experience. I could loiter where
I pleased, stare at all and sundry, have obscene conversations over beer about fictional debauches with peach-
thighed girls, I could even stand facing a tree trunk and
fiddle with my fly, pretending to be scandalously relieving
myself in a public place in broad daylight, with two young
women not twenty yards away, turning scarlet and talking
with a great deal of liveliness.

I could do all that, forbidden even to the boldest Joan,
but I had come so far now from the terrible day on the
tram that there were times, staring boldly into a face, or

boldly pretending to adjust my private parts where I pretended they were hanging in the private darkness of those pants: there were times when all this lost its savor. No one really looked, no one stared or cared, I was just another man. Then I wanted to rip off my jacket and thrust what bosom I could at these potato-faced people who did not guess, and have them gasp and turn purple, fall at my feet dead of apoplexy and scandal, and to cry: *You fools, do you not see I am Joan, making history?*

I was not slow now, but among the quickest between the tables, and it was second nature now to line six plates up along my arms, and remember who wanted his chop extra well done and who had been particular about no gravy. I forgot nothing, dropped nothing, was no longer a hopeless incompetent bungler with plates of scones no one wanted. There was a pleasure in becoming nothing more than a machine, the pleasure of directing the body and the brain, that was a pleasure like no other.

Until at last that, like my disguise, was too good. Who would have thought I could be too good? But I became bored with my skill with six plates, and everyone else was more impressed than I was with my grasp of detail about gravy, and my memory for the details of chops and faces. I was bored with myself and with my excellence.

It was then that I began to think of Duncan, imagined him down for some livestock show or other, stiff in his awful tweed coat and the tie he looked choked in, his city outfit. He would be happy after a day of looking at the hairy swinging tassels of bulls and the imbecile cows with their ballooning udders: down for the sales and making the best of things, having had a laugh or two with a mate or two in a bar or two, and later, by himself, in need of a chop. He would be a man content with his life, after a fashion, but with a set of furrows on his face put there by the precipitous departure of Joan some time before. I did not like to dwell on how my disappearance might have hurt Duncan. Instead I liked the vision of a man smelling of a few beers and the sweat of a day of bulls, and he would turn into this convenient corner chophouse and not glance up in giving his order to the waiter. Or perhaps he would, perhaps he would glance up at the waiter, standing there with the order book in her hand and the pencil grown cumbersome in her fingers: perhaps he would glance up and history would be made afresh.

To be loved and to love in return, I was beginning to see, was a kind of history too: while to be alone, secretive, a presser of my palm against glass panes, looking out at life, was history of a kind I did not much want to make. I saw all the people passing and sitting and talking and eating their chops and wiping their moustaches, and I saw the way their mouths turned down, and I was afraid mine might be starting to. They were unloved, or un-loving, or both: they were those whose wives had made fools of them and cuckolded them in their own beds, they were those whose husbands had tired of them and courted their angel-skinned young sisters: they were those whose fathers had abandoned them, whose mothers had banged their infant heads against the wall, those whose parents had never smiled, but had prayed overmuch and run the world on sin and retribution.

Those eaters of chops, lonely men who did not know how to do for themselves, bumbling bachelors with their buttons hanging by threads, seemed to have few stories of bliss and requited love, or did not wish to share them with an expressionless waiter holding a grubby napkin. But they had tales of betrayal or rejection, and I listened to many of them.

There are no rational reasons for loving, my regular Edgar announced. He was a good tipper and a late-night customer, so for those reasons he was a chop-eater I listened to as he held forth to the faceless waiter. Edgar, a pale pudgy type of man, greasy of cuff like most of the chop-eaters but younger than most of the sad beaten men here, and with something of passion in his eyes, had thought in detail about love. *If you love,* he told me, gnawing on his bit of singed chop bone, *let me tell you what can happen, logically speaking. The object of your love can ignore or reject you. Result: misery. Or she can accept you until you are helpless with love, and then turn on you. Result: misery. You yourself can tire of your love and have to disentangle yourself. Result: guilt if you are a gentleman, inconvenience if you are a cad. Or she can accept you and go on doing so, and you can go on loving her. Result: dread of the death of your loved one, or her change of heart. Net result of any of these: a negative balance or debit. Who would love, then?*

His eyes, rather too far apart for the comfort of anyone looking at them, seemed filmy with the hopelessness of his logic, and as a mere waiter, keen on a tip and tired at the end of a day full of plates and faces, I had no answer for him.

The more right he seemed, though, the more wrong I felt him to be. Other men wept openly into their cups of sweet tea and their chops, and told me their terrible stories of pain at the hands of love, and somehow they were more right than chalky Edgar, ticking points off on his sharp fingers and wiping the grease off his mouth in a conclusive sort of way.

His words set me to dreaming, though, and Duncan's face came to me more frequently in those long nights. In my dreams I saw that he was dryer, sandier, skinnier, and more angular than ever, his ankles loose in their sockets. In my dreams I watched from above as he walked up to my front door, and I could see a furrow between his sandy eyebrows that had never been there before. I watched him hesitate at the door and glance behind him, hitch up his pants like a person who has to remind himself of his manhood, and quickly, as if in fear of changing his mind, reach out to press the doorbell. What a pealing and ringing echoed around me! And where was I, that there was no door from this room so I could descend and open the door to my Duncan? And when I turned from seeking a door, where had the window gone? The pealing clashed around me and I could hear Duncan calling: *Joanie, Joanie,* with a melancholy sound like wind, but from my dry mouth not the smallest sound could be made to emerge, to answer him. I woke in tears of despair, trembling in the dawn, with the image of Duncan gone, never to return. *Come back, Duncan, come back!* It was a grief and anxiety like to choke me, and I had to spring from that suffocating bed and stand watching the grubby dawn above the roof across the way.

I had despised love and had turned away from it when I had had a glut of it: I had not suffered. Now, in the grip of dreams of regret, I began to know what I had cast away so easily. Each morning dawned and I woke alone, each evening fell without my soul having touched the soul of another: I was free, I was a woman of independent flight, I could walk along any street and, from my splendid start at the Galaxy—because it truly had been an independent step—I could carry out many destinies, even some of the ones I had invented. All that was grand, and I treasured it: but it was hollow too, and at the heart of that life there was nothing more than I, Joan, a soul spinning quite alone.

It is women who are supposed to moon and languish and fill their days with love and scheming, but it was as a man that I softened and grew fluid, reconsidering the notion of love. I was a man with a cross face (I caught glimpses of myself in the windows of shops and saw how surly I looked) standing in a smell of roasting chop with a soiled napkin over his arm, concealing his heart from the world as he concealed his breasts.

I waited for Duncan to hanker for that chop, but he seemed not to fancy it, or was eating it elsewhere, and the day came when I was oppressed past bearing by the whole dark paraphernalia of being a man. It seemed like no kind of history at all, just another meaningless folly of pride, and I was pricked at last to take action.

It had seemed desperate and urgent while the pen was putting words on paper, but when the letter had slid into the slit and I had heard it fall with a silky sound on to others, bills and *billets-doux,* I wondered. I wondered if he would consider replying to the invitation of his remorseful but perhaps unforgivable wife, who had made such a fool of him in front of his stockmen and blacks, and had humiliated him as only a wife can humiliate the husband who loves her. I wondered if Duncan's face had grown bitter under his hat, rasped daily by thoughts of his wife, whose image—my image—was perhaps now one of loathing and gall.

I had hurt Duncan, done violence to his real feelings for me, but I consoled myself with the thought that I had spared him the worst, most degrading memories. In sliding away from between jars of peas in brine, I had made a fool of him, yes. But I had not subjected him to the memory of having begged, pleaded, gone down on his knees and clutched me to make me stay. I had not debased him that far. I had reduced him to tears, no doubt, but private ones, hot tears shed in the pain of empty rooms. He did not have to remember weeping and shouting, begging me to stay, and he did not have to remember any expression of distaste or pity on the face of the stony-hearted wife waiting for his pleas to stop. I was glad to have spared him that, for there is dignity in grief, but there can be no dignity in the degradation of one begging with tears on his cheeks for a woman to stay who has made up her mind to go.

Nights began to be endless and white, dawns became unforgiving. I stood in my boardinghouse room listening to the world wake, to birds making their rackets from trees, dogs warning off dew, the quick smug footsteps of early risers along the road. I stood, and even more than in the stretches of the interminable night I could not imagine what it was all about. I thought of Duncan at those times, and thought of my letter being unfolded by his fingers, and read by his eyes. I remembered all the violent dawns I had witnessed from his window, and found myself uttering small moaning noises of reconsideration, of regret and remorse. *What is it all about?* I whispered to the window. *What have I done?* My despair fogged the glass, and I could remember that someone, some earnest person or other in my madcap youth, had asked me the same question, and had inspected my face at length, exhaustingly, waiting for an answer. And what had I answered? I wished I could remember now, because I could remember that I had found an answer in the end that had satisfied us: but in my madcap youth I had had answers for all the hard questions, while now I seemed to have none at all.

JOAN MAKES HISTORY

SCENE NINE

In 1878 the name on everyone's lips was that of
Ned Kelly, the bushranger who was to become the
country's greatest hero. I, Joan, captured his
likeness, and that of his gang, for posterity,
although it was only after the event that I realized
I had been in the same room as a legend.

STANDING in a black bag would never have been my idea of a life. There I was, though, in a dusty black bag with my eye to cold glass, inspecting faces as they stood before me. *Chin up,* I called, my voice muffled by all the black fabric. *Chin up, thanks, and relax that left hand if you don't mind.*

I had tried it myself, of course. I had felt my neck go rigid against the headrest and my face go wooden as I stood with my hand on the broken plaster column or sat in the imposing carved chair that was held together at the back with a few brave pieces of string. I had itched with wanting to move, and from behind the black cloth I had heard Alfred's muffled voice: *Chin up, dearie, and stick out your front a bit more.*

It was a sideline, Alfred's suggestive cards, and it was the condition on which I had got the job. *Can't abide to have a female working for me,* Alfred had said. *But you'll do if you'll pose, dearie.* I stood then, showing a bit of ankle, a bit of rounded shoulder, a coquettishly out-thrust bosom (covered, I hasten to assure, with a certain bead-fringed tasselled bodice that Alfred had found to have inflammatory effects on those who handed over their cash for my poses, and cunningly padded to give

197

a bit of what I lacked in the way of endowment). Being plain of feature, I had been astonished when Alfred made his suggestion to me, assuming in my innocence that a comely face was essential to the satisfaction of the unknown gents who clutched my image in front of them in the dim privacy of their bedrooms. I soon enough discovered, though, that faces were not important to those men: what mattered was the angle of the knee and ankle as I bent forward over a carelessly revealed stocking top and a troublesome garter, or the smooth curve of my shoulder as I half-concealed and half-revealed behind a large feather fan. *Your face!* Alfred had exclaimed with a rude laugh, early on, when I had expressed wonderment that my face would be suitable for this task. *You do not think, dearie, that it is your face they are looking at, do you?* I swallowed my feelings: for a few mad moments I had thought my face, my plain bane all my life, had found an appreciative audience, and I was only slightly pained to learn how totally irrelevant it was to anyone, possibly, but myself.

I did wonder, at times, if my poor abandoned Henry ever consoled himself with the small round-cornered cards from which Alfred made such a profit. If he did, had he ever looked at the face there on the pose, as well as the thigh or shoulder? I had come to feel differently about Henry, though, and missed him sorely; I had even tried writing him a letter.

The posing was not a pleasure to me, as it might have been to another, and Alfred told me that it was to my advantage that I did not relish it. *The sluts that love to flaunt themselves are unworkmanlike,* he said. *They will not keep still, and they fancy themselves to have temperament,* Alfred snorted. *I cannot abide them,* he said with feeling. *I loathe them.* Alfred was most workmanlike at his posed cards, and it was clear to me early on that he was an expert, with a cool judging eye for a provocative detail, because he himself was quite unprovoked by female flesh. Whether boys or goats were capable of inflaming his pasty flesh I did not care to ascertain, but it made the whole chilly process of flesh-flaunting more tolerable, to know that he saw me as nothing more than a pattern of light and shade that would bring him a few more guineas.

Posing, then, was part of it, but I felt the other part to be more worthy of me: the hours spent hovering seductively over my garter were tedious, but those spent in the back room or under the black cloth were not. In the back room, mixing the collodion for the plates, I felt I had a hand in the machinery of life, as I never felt I had before, when I was simply the wife of Henry.

It was not all that different, I had to admit: it was kitchen sort of work, mixing and stirring, spreading and pouring and wiping, but with substances less friendly than flour and sugar. The gun cotton was explosive, the acid could strip flesh from bone, the fumes of the simmering nitrate-of-silver made my head ache, and the cyanide for the fixing made me half sick. It was dangerous work, and smelly, and necessitated a stained leather apron, but I was proud of the hallmark of my profession, my nitrate-blackened fingers, and felt myself part of a special secret aristocracy of people who knew how to catch a bit of the world and make it stick to a piece of glass.

Alfred saw no magic in it now, if he ever had, but I watched as he fiddled with the rosewood box where the transformation of chemicals into visible soul took place, and he saw my interest. On dull grey days when the light was poor and custom was slow, he showed me all the mysteries of levers and tiny brass gimcracks. *You are quick to catch on, I will say that for you,* he said, and seemed pleased to let me fiddle on my own, and then take a portrait or two of himself, leaning on the back of a chair looking peeved, for that was the expression his face took in repose.

I was lucky, having fallen on my feet with Alfred. Because I did the posing, which brought him in so many guineas, as well as all the mixing and measuring, and because he was a man with an unusual sense of fairness, he paid me a sum sufficient to keep body and soul together. I thanked Providence, for I knew that most employers feigned to think such a thing against nature and the laws of commerce, and claimed that the world would collapse forthwith if a woman were able to feed and shelter herself from nothing but her own labor. I counted myself absurdly lucky, knowing that without such an eccentric employer I would be slaving over needles and poor thread far into the night and slowly starving, like most females who lived without a man.

We did all manner of people in our studio: we did fine society folk in satin and silk, squatters in toppers, and any number of wooden brides clutching posies. We did grocers and paperhangers, we did the Fire Brigade cricket team and the St Jude's Memorial Brass Band. But the ones I relished most were the rough fellows from the bush with their angular wives and open-mouthed children.

A whole tribe of them clattered up the stairs to the studio one day, several large bearded men with wide leather belts holding up their moleskins, several women as skinny as myself, and a troop of children. They were from *up Glenrowan way,* they told us, as if we were interested, and the oldest woman, a gaunt creature in black who might once have been an Irish beauty, put a handful of notes on the table and said they wanted them *took, the whole gang, separate and together.*

They were not quite the usual kind of customer: they did not take us aside to insist how we must conceal their saucerlike ears, or their children's gigantic noses, but they were also vain in their own ways, and were determined not to be made small by any mere machine.

The tallest of the young men was the first to face the cold eye of the camera. He seemed somewhat the dandy, in a primitive way: with his moleskins he wore an incongruous green sash that he was at pains to display, and he had been careful to wet his hair and comb it up from his forehead so there was no missing his rather fine eyes. Alfred showed him all our backdrops and props. *I can recommend the sylvan glade, sir, for a country gentleman like yourself,* he urged, but this rustic was not going to be made mock of by Alfred. He wished to face the camera from the Gentleman's Library, with its square of dummy books behind him, an elbow on a gilt-edged volume of Shakespeare, and the ornate gilded legs of the desk concealing the stand of the headrest. *This is a nasty contraption,* he said when Alfred guided his head into it, and seemed unable to abide the feel of it around the back of his neck. *Allow me, sir,* Alfred said, and settled him against it again with his rather finicky gestures, but that made the customer push him off and get his head into the metal by himself, and stand there straddle-legged leaning on Shakespeare and sizing up Alfred with bold contemptuous eyes, so that the poor man became somewhat flustery and had to take refuge under the black cloth. *Just relax those hands, sir,* he called from the safety of his cloth, but this fellow with the sash seemed a man forever on his guard, and when the shutter clicked his fists were still clenched.

The older woman seemed to be doing this for posterity rather than pleasure, and stared grimly out of the sylvan glade as if about to be executed. Alfred had a bit of palaver for when his female customers chose the sylvan glade, but he did not try to tell this thin-lipped stony

201

person that she was for all the world like a wood nymph. The young women, who in spite of their best silk skirts moved with heavy efficient cow-herding steps, like men, entered into the spirit of the thing, leaning against the chaise longue smiling somewhat stiffly, with a palm behind them and a fan throttled in their large capable hands.

The children were rough creatures who had been buttoned and strapped into frills and sailor suits they were plainly new to and plainly loathed. They could not get the hang of looking natural with one foot up on a lobster pot, or leaning against a plaster pillar. The family cajoled from the sidelines, urging with shouted witticisms that made the children look more cranky than ever: even the reminder that future generations would pore over these photographs did not cheer up those children.

They were a hard morning's work, this lot, and when they had taken their loud voices and heavy boots down the stairs, Alfred lay for a short while on the chaise longue while I tidied the chaos of lobster pots and fans, and made up more glass plates, for this family from *up Glenrowan way* had used our whole supply.

So our next customer took us by surprise, walking up the stairs silently and coming across Alfred taking his ease. I was behind the camera with my chamois, but I could hear this customer discussing his needs with Alfred, and I went stiff behind the box and looked hard at the way the groove in every tiny brass screw that held it together had been aligned perfectly vertical, and I thought of the satisfaction some tidy dry-handed man had enjoyed, getting every screw right, and at a very great distance I could hear Alfred saying, *Full-length, then, is it sir?* and the reply: *Yes, full length, it is to send to my mother back Home, and she will not believe unless she sees my entire person.*

It was I who had created this situation, I who had written, but in spite of that I wished Alfred would send me to the back room to mix or cut or wash, and himself stand behind the camera and take his gentleman's whole person for his mother back Home. Just this once I had no wish to arrange hands and cane and feet at the right angle, and position the headrest so it did not show, and call out encouragingly about looking into the middle distance and not breathing.

I slipped away to the back room and tried to busy myself among the shelves and jars, although there was nothing to do there, and could hear Alfred getting his gentleman in position, being polite about taking his chin in his fingers: *Chin up a fraction if you please, sir, and relax, you do not want your mother to see you looking too grave about it all, do you, sir?* I heard laughter as he tried to set the gentleman at ease, and I stared at the dishes where I mixed the collodion, feeling how very cold my fingers were, and how hard I was suddenly finding it to breathe: how, although I had pictured this moment often enough, now that it was upon me I had gone numb and uncertain.

It was not like me to remain in the back room when a customer was present, since I was a person of curiosity, and Alfred knew how I enjoyed the pushing and prodding of hapless folk, gone limp before the camera's cold eye, into stances suitable for recording forever. He gave me a look when he came in, but I busied myself with a cork in a jar and he did not remark on anything as together we prepared the nitrate and the developing box. But before he dipped the plate in the nitrate he said, *Joan, just go and see that he is still in position, would you be so good?* and with my frozen brain I could think of no pretext for not going, no pretext except falling down in a faint, and that would be sure to bring the customer in to help, and I would be further into my problem.

I went out, then, feeling that my heart would pound its way out of my chest, and got under the black bag as swiftly as I could, and without looking at the man standing on the puckered rug. Under the bag, looking out through the lens, I began to breathe again, panting so the glass fogged over and I had to move back, but I had seen that the position in which Alfred had put this gentleman was in profile to the camera, for he was possessed, of course, of a fine profile, and being a conscientious sort of man— oh, how conscientious and careful!—had obeyed what Alfred had said, and not moved a muscle. He stood, then, staring sideways off into the middle distance, and had not even allowed his eyes to swivel around when I came into the room.

Many muddled things went through my mind, a blur of thoughts too quick to catch, like the blur of head that Mrs Ramsgate had been when she had sneezed at the vital moment: out of this blur I wished to speak, and wished to make the profile turn to me. *Very good, sir,* I called at last. *Excellent, just hold that, sir, for a minute longer.* My voice emerged muffled from the thick black cloth and the gentleman on the rug did not move: there might have been an additional stiffening of his already stiff figure, but I could not be sure of that, and in any case Alfred had come out from the back room, impatient with the delay, and bustled me out from the camera, and then there was the whole fast business of the nitrate-dipping, and the speeding of the plate to the camera, the crackling flare of the magnesium, and the racing of the plate back to the developing box.

You watch it, dearie, Alfred said, *and I will unlock the poor gent.* I was left alone in the back room with the glass plate in its box, and as I put my eye to the peephole,

there, sure enough, faint as a ghost but becoming stronger
as the moments passed, were the boots, the cane, the
large firm hands, the best wing collar and tie, and yes,
there it was, the face which I could not bring myself to
look at immediately: the face of my Henry. When once
I had made myself look at his face I could not then make
myself stop, and was still crouching over the peephole
when Alfred came back in. *Is he not cooked yet, Joan
dearie?* Alfred asked, and nudged me aside to look: *Goodness, he is well and truly done,* he said, and made haste
to remove the plate from the box. *Do the money, would
you please Joan,* he said, and like a machine I went out
to Henry.

Henry in person, unlocked from the headrest and the
gaze of the lens, stood by the table where people paid.
Well, Joanie, he said in an odd sort of voice, glancing
at me quickly and then away as if I dazzled like the sun.
I received your letter, as you can see. He shot me a ghostly
small smile that was unsure of its welcome. *And here I
am.* He bit off anything more: all the things he might
have asked, such as how long I had been here, did I like
it, and was I the paramour of Albert? I saw him frame
all these questions to himself and bite them all off, and
I recognized him in that moment as intimately as I
recognized myself mirrored unexpectedly in shop windows: I knew his every frailty and every strength.

This moment silenced me: I, garrulous Joan, always
ready with a quick bit of an answer, could find not a
single word to put my tongue to, except one. *Henry,* I
said, and the word unlocked something that rolled over
me like the breaking of waters.

JOAN

I *did my best to loathe you,* Duncan said above the clatter of the train. *I filled my heart with images of you and poured hatred over them.* Outside the window, the sun dazzled from small bodies of water, paddocks passed laboriously, sheep ran away in a fluster with their silly fallen-down-stockings of legs, cows stared and chewed, and a band of sunlight took turns to lie across Duncan's lap and then mine.

I felt my fingers to be still greasy and dark from such a number of plates, knives, forks, and felt my feet still puffy from such a lot of standing, keeping a watchful eye on the table near the door from which a couple of lads had once made a quick exit without paying. And how strange and naked I felt with my legs bare under a skirt! How odd it felt to be without my shoes with the laces, and the socks with clocks on them!

Who was the impostor? The man Jack whose husk I had left behind, or this shorn-looking woman watching the sunlight sliding from her lap to that of the man opposite? I had abandoned Jack in a suitcase outside the Salvation Army: Jack had folded himself up among the jackets and ties and the socks with clocks on them, and it was Joan who had locked the door of the room for

209

the last time and slid the key under Mrs Elliot's door. I sat fingering the cloth of my new skirt: I was Joan now, and Joan was no more an impostor than Jack had been. Under all skirts and socks with clocks I was everyone who had ever breathed, sat, made errors of judgment: and there was Duncan, who was also no impostor, but every good man who had ever forgiven a fool.

I tried, Joanie, and succeeded for a while, Duncan said. The band of sun lay between us while I pictured Duncan smiling, gesturing, caressing some other woman's shoulder, waxing carnal late at night after a drop or two taken. Such things were no doubt true, but it did not seem necessary to linger on such truths: I felt there were things more important than the truths of the recent history of Duncan and myself. *But hating is hard work, I found.* Duncan had grown a few grey hairs among the sandy ones, and had acquired a line on either side of his mouth, and one between his eyebrows, that had not been there before, but the freckles on his lips and his pebble-colored eyes were still the same. *But Duncan, where are we going?* I asked, for I had boarded the train in a blur, seeing nothing but Duncan's tweed back in the crowd, carrying the case with the few things I wanted from Jack's life. *Ah, Joanie, you must let me surprise you,* Duncan said now, and winked, although he did not smile: I had not seen him smile yet. *I promise you a surprise,* he said, *and I think you will find it worth the wait.*

I could not quite gauge this new Duncan, for the old one had been so full of soft looks, and had liked to be in contact with my flesh whenever possible (so that, for example, in the old days had we sat facing each other like this, he would have made sure his shoe was up alongside mine, or our knees rubbing each other through cloth): so this Duncan, who did not smile (although he did not frown, either), and who did not touch me (though

he did not seem to be avoiding me either), was strange
to me, although the way he called me *Joanie* (only my
husband ever called me *Joanie*) was something I found
reassuring.

I will be patient, then, Duncan, I said, and moved my
leg in such a way that my knee was about to come in
contact with his, but at that instant he leaned forward
to the window so that his knee was again separated from
mine by a hand's-breadth of air. *We are off, Joanie, off
we go,* he said, and I heard the excitement in his voice,
and could not guess whether or not he had avoided my
touch.

I wished for no kind of conversation: there was no
small-beer information-exchanging kind of dialogue I
wished to have. Our separate pasts were foreign languages:
no matter what details I had found, to describe my life
as Jack, no matter what he had told me of his life as
Duncan-by-himself, nothing but the crudest facts could
have been conveyed. And what was the point of primitive
chunks of fact? What was real about being Jack or being
Duncan-by-himself was not the facts, but the feelings,
and such kinds of truths could not be spoken of in a
rattling train trundling over paddocks full of bandy-legged
silly sheep.

So we gazed out at those sheep and at gum trees bending
under wind we could not feel and at bedrock exposed in
cuttings. Small towns fled past our window: I leaned
forward and strained to read the names on their stations,
but they were a blur, and in any case my grasp of
geography had never been great, and whether we had
been heading towards the coast or towards the junction
of the western rivers, the names of the towns would not
have helped me to know our direction.

And what difference could it make? I assumed we were
returning by some roundabout route or other to that place

of dust and dryness, where sunrise had become a chronic affliction to me. This time I was prepared to learn the language of that place: secretively I watched Duncan's profile as he gazed out at Australia passing, and in my mind a picture grew of the Joan I could be if I took the leap of imagination I had been too purblind to take last time. This time, instead of laughing at the lists of cows Father sent me—*Santa Gertrudis, Belted Galloway, Blonde d'Aquitane*—I would learn my own lists, learn the names and needs of the dusty brown mobs Duncan owned. I would learn to get up on the back of a horse, and imagined the exhilaration of leaping fences, and of camping at night with Duncan beside me and the stars blazing just above our heads. I had got the hang of scones with Elsie, and knew what worth I would find in the floury Country Women's Association women, now that I had an inkling of what to look for: I would grow lean, brown, perhaps even a little leathery of complexion; I would at last know how to live the life that had been given to me, having had a go at living one or two others.

In the meantime I was reconciled to waiting and to silence and, after all, Duncan had never been anything but a silent man. Of course my own pride would have been better served (since it was I who had approached Duncan and pleaded for another chance), had Duncan gone down on his knees before me, covered my feet with kisses, become wild-eyed and ardent, but I was more humble now than I had once been, and was prepared to be patient.

Morning wore on, and our band of sliding sun grew shorter and shorter and disappeared at last. We stopped now and again at the larger towns, and it was the third or fourth of these, as the train slid in and stopped with a sigh, that Duncan stood, stretched, and looked down at me. *I will forage us up a bite to eat, Joanie,* he said.

What do you say? I watched him stride down the platform towards Refreshments, feeling a little cheered: Duncan was not going to cover my feet with kisses, but I felt somewhat cherished by this foraging. I sat staring at the train across the platform, where I could see an old woman reading a book with a magnifying glass, and was reassured that there would be a new life with Duncan, and that affection would, in time, blossom again.

But there was a humming expectant quality to the silence of our train that began to make me anxious. I felt stifled by the silence: it seemed as though Duncan and I were the only passengers on this entire train, and the old woman the only passenger on the other. The platform was completely empty and I began to peer out of the window, pressing my cheek against its dirty glass, and wished I had looked at my watch as Duncan had left, for now I was having to tell myself that, although it felt that he had been gone an hour, it could not be so.

In the silence a man in a uniform startled me by walking past the window inches from my eye: I heard a distant whistle: I stared at the woman with the magnifying glass and told myself that the train was not moving yet. But it would be moving soon, we had been here forever, and where was Duncan, and what would happen if the train left him behind?

As this thought came to me it was engulfed by another, which filled my mind like a picture of truth: a picture of Duncan not returning to the train before it left the station, but watching as I was carried off: watching not in dismay, not wildly wondering if he could leap on it as it gathered speed, but watching with glee. I saw it all: Duncan reading my letter, tearing it up, then thinking better of it: getting the bits out of the fireplace to piece together the address at the top, and standing at the window tapping his fingers on the glass, smiling at the thought of his revenge.

How neat it would be, how entirely fitting! I, Joan, would be swept on to whatever town was next, without a ticket, without any idea where I was, without any life I could return to, having sold up everything: there I would be with nothing, Duncan making a fool of me much more elegantly than I had made a fool of him.

As I pictured all this I knew it to be true and I leaped to my feet determined to avoid the trap while there was still time. At the door of our carriage I glanced up and down the empty platform and across at the other train: there, framed in the window with the woman with the magnifying glass, I saw Duncan. *Ah,* I thought, *you fox, you are returning the way we came, not to be caught!* I sprang across the platform and up into the other carriage, bounced from wall to wall down the corridor and burst into the compartment of the old lady: she looked up from her book and dropped the magnifying glass with the shock of my precipitous arrival: the man with her stared too, and frowned: another man altogether, a man with small blue eyes and a cleft in his chin, a man not in the least like Duncan.

Then he must be hiding there on the station! I leaped off the train, feeling it start to move under me, and tried to run, forgetting the clinging skirt and the awkward flimsy shoes: got to Refreshments and flung the door back so hard it rebounded off a table and sprang closed against me: pushed it again and saw a red-faced man with white whiskers standing like a demonstration of patience, monumental beside a gleaming tea urn. Duncan was not here: I heard whistles from behind me on the platform: I heard a man's voice yelling words I could not understand: out on the platform the train, our train, was sliding coyly along the platform: I ran towards it, and there, his hat fallen over his eyes, his mouth laughing under it, with paper cups and brown paper bags spilling from his hands, was Duncan, panting as we both somehow got on to the train. *Joanie, I have never missed a train in my life, there was no danger whatsoever, I assure you,* Duncan panted, and at last, after so many cautious un-smiling days with each other, our skins unwarmed by the touch of another skin, it was there in the swaying doorway that we embraced at last, and laughed together to see the rock cakes tumble out the door.

I was right in thinking Duncan had a surprise for me, but it was not the cruel surprise I had pictured. The surprise was that Duncan did not take me to that place of challenging sunrises, but to a house in the city by the sea where I had had all my beginnings. *This is where I live now,* he said. *I am a man of business now, such as you yourself have been,* and we had a good laugh together over that.

It was not long before a giant began to grow within me, kicking and dancing, chuckling at the way I exclaimed at the feel of feet against me. It was a benign giant, and one I already loved for carrying the face of that man Duncan, my husband again, and now after so long the man I loved. He lay beside me in sleep, a rounded fetus shape himself under the bedclothes, breathing the steady breaths of a sleeper who knows he is being watched with eyes full of love.

What was the moment I loved best? Ah, bear with me while I indulge myself, thinking of the moment I loved best. It was when he lay beside me, my skin touching and whispering to his, and the birds outside warbling in a watery way about the new morning they were enjoying. He lay knowing I was there, not yet awake, but not still asleep either, and he knew even through his closed eyes that I was watching him in a passion of tenderness that

brought the tears prickling to my eyes. What I watched
was his mouth, the faint smile at its corners that told
me he knew I was watching, and he knew I was smiling
too, and he could feel my love coming through my skin
to him, so that when at last he opened his eyes he was
already smiling.

But I had made a bad sort of bargain, I saw now, too
late. I had had love, I had had adoration, I had had a
soul who would have gone on his knees before me: I had
had the devotion of a good man. Before I had abandoned
him, Duncan's eyes had always grown soft with private
bliss, staring at me so that I grew uneasy, loud, brutal
under his adoring gaze. He had brought me gifts: not a
week had passed that his eye had not been caught by
some little trinket or some bit of frippery he knew would
please me. He had been proud of me, had been proud
to be the husband of Joan, the woman to whom he had
entirely made over his heart. I had enjoyed all this, but
had I seen the worth of his love? Had I known how rare
and how fragile such a thing was, and did I worry myself
with ways to make sure it did not fade? No! I, Joan, had
been a fool, let me not mince words. Duncan had adored
me, and I had scorned him so much, regarded him so
little, that I had done that cruel thing of making a monkey
of him at the Show. I had watched him then and not
softened: I had not been able even to imagine what he
felt, the panic and despair in the mornings, waking up
alone.

Now I was paying for all that. For Duncan and I were
there, husband and wife, about to be the father and
mother of someone or other, but Duncan was no longer
that man who adored me. Duncan now was a man whose
eyes tended to slide away when they met mine, who could
submerge into long silences in which I had no part, who
did not reach for my hand as we strolled along beaches

or pavements. He let me take his hand, he even gave it a squeeze or two, but his heart was not in the palm of my hand, as once it had been: he was now someone with a membrane around himself.

I was frightened of words, having used too many in my life, too glibly, rolled great numbers of them together into constructions of deceit. On such sweet mornings with Duncan, I tried out some in my mind, for the press of feeling demanded outlet, and I went through all the worn-out phrases I had heard, the suspect phrases about love and passion and for ever and ever. I tasted them but they frightened me still, and were sullied by all the other times they had filled the earholes of trusting men and women who had wept in bitterness later, finding the words hollow. So all I could do to relieve the press of my painful tenderness was to make a sound that I heard with surprise was a sort of groan or moan, and touch with a finger that trembled slightly that bit of cheek pushed back by the small secret smile of my husband.

Are eyes the windows of the soul? I asked one morning, staring into his. I asked that somewhat theatrical question when what I would really have liked to do would be to speak of my good fortune and the awe in which I held it. I would have liked to find the words for my gratitude and amazement that I was now exchanging love with the eyes of this man, and feeling his giant dancing within me, instead of eating the savorless bread of lonely pride.

Duncan was too wise to listen too closely to anything as sly as words, and wrapped his long arms around me, so I sighed with the bliss of being held tight by him. After some time he said, *Yes, they are the windows and doorways and gravel driveways and gateposts with lions, if you want,* and we lay in silence then, for it did not matter what words passed between us.

Now, as I had never done before, I worried about death, although not my own. Now that I knew Duncan again, I could not envisage life without him, and like any fond and foolish lovelorn girl I brought a cold sweat of dread to my skin, imagining him lying dead and knowing he would never open his eyes and slide a bony arm around me. *Is there a price to pay for every damn thing?* I cried at him, and Duncan, wise man, did not answer, for not knowing what I meant, but seeing some rage in me that did not make sense.

My sleep now was full of dreams: I dreamed that I lay curled like a tight green bud in a warm green room with walls made of leaves: I dreamed of sailing among islands that closed in until they formed a tunnel that I did not notice until it was too late. I dreamed of all the men on the station: Duncan, the men in hats, and the black stockmen, all lined up while I cut their hair with a pair of scissors made in the shape of a stork.

I remembered the last time I had felt myself growing full of someone else, when the whole thing had seemed a prison, so that I had grown frantic and blind like a hysterical cat in a bag. How different all things were now! I had looked into the face of destiny and found it cold: I envied no one now, hankered after no greatness, dreamed no dreams of crowds cheering my name, armies following where I led, the ardor of artists inspired by my face: all that was an empty mockery, while sitting with my feet up, dreaming away the days and nights in a smudge of sentiment, seemed a finer thing to do than any of those.

I would never have believed that it would have been enough history for me to grow huge and sluggish, gaping at nothing and whispering in my heart to the small being within me. *Women!* I would have scorned, *It is all lies and believing what other people tell you!* and I despised them for knowing what a matinee jacket was, and how

218

to deal with a nappy pin. But small affairs of nappies and names were beginning to interest me, after scorning so long the small pink hams in cribs over which mothers crowed and clucked.

I had taken to smiling a great deal: my face had never been the sort to shape itself easily around soft emotions, but now when I caught sight of myself in mirrors or felt the muscles on my face operating from within, a yellow buttery-smooth smile was usually happening on my cheeks.

I dreamed and gazed at nothing, and could spend a whole day at a time moving an item or two from one room to another. I mused, full of happiness: although there were also times when I woke sweating from foul dreams of blood and grief, and sprang out of bed as fast as my bulk would let me to stop the memory of the last time.

Duncan never spoke of the last time: our silence on that event was profound. But he coddled me with tepid eggs, and tempted me with delicacies out of brown paper bags. He had not forgotten during my embittering absence what it was that could tempt me.

Duncan's pride in his shapeless wife, his wife in various bags of flowered cotton, was frightening, as if the bulge I carried under my ribs, the source of his pride, was something apart from me. There were times when I had to fight a pang of envy for the creature inside me, which was untainted, and so someone he could love without reservation. Perhaps he guessed, for he would whisper, *Ah Joanie, you are magnificent,* and his hand would move over whatever part of my bloated body was closest.

He smiled over me and his face went gaunt with pleasure when he laid his palm on the bulge of tight skin under which that new person lay: when his hand did this, timidly, for the first time, I saw his face go pale. *I am already doting,* he said after a moment and laughed.

He had more words, but they stuck in his throat, I heard him choke on his own doting, and I lay with my eyes full of tears. I, cool Joan, woman of destiny, was reduced like all the women I had laughed at to a bulging mother-to-be in washed-out cotton flowers, filled with sentimental tears and squeezing tight the hot hand of her husband.

JOAN MAKES HISTORY

SCENE TEN

During the 1890s Australia suffered a calamitous
depression which wise men thought should be left
to the natural workings of the marketplace. In the
art which captured the picturesque distress of those
people slowly starving, I, Joan, found a permanent
place.

KEN was a good man, with a strong right arm with an axe, and I had married him knowing that my plain face could not expect a miracle in the way of a man, and knowing that a good man with an axe, and a man whose large warm hands were honest in what they did and a comfort when they squeezed mine, was a good prospect for a lifetime together. *I am no great shakes, Joanie,* he had said, watching the backs of those freckled hands of his while he proposed. I smiled and hung my head modestly, but I also said what I believed: *I am no great shakes either, Ken, you are good enough for me.*

In the end it seemed no great shakes to stay where we were in Budgeree, with Ken coming home to our hut at night, silent with the tiredness of having chopped all day for someone else, or even worse, the gloom of having tramped from place to place and found no one who wanted his strong arms. It was on the day of rest, after the kneeling and creaking together under the blast of heat from the roof, that he came out of his silence and said *You know, Joanie, I have been giving it some thought.* We had been man and wife for long enough now that I knew better than to be impatient and ask, *What, Ken, what have you been giving thought?* I knew by now that

223

Ken could be as slow as a bit of grass growing, and that it was necessary to be patient and wait until he was ready to speak.

We walked up the dusty track in a throb of cicadas and I pretended Ken had not spoken, so I would not be impatient to hear what he would say next. Patience was not in my nature, I was always a woman of fire and flame, slow deliberation was not my style. But I had learned at last that Ken was not to be hurried, that he closed down into silence altogether if harassed to speak, and I had learned a few tricks of patience, and was at last rewarded now with what he had been thinking. *See, there is no future for us here,* he said, and I pressed back the words wanting to spring from my mind, because he had more to say, and I did not want to frighten his speech away by being impetuous. *Plenty of water this time of year,* he said out of another long silence. *And I can get any amount of wild tucker.*

I had not only learned patience, outlasting the long thinking silences of my husband, but I was learning ingenuity too, to follow all the gaps in the slow stream of his ideas. I was ahead of him, already on the road, when he said loudly, *We will get on the road, I reckon, and do a bit better for ourselves somewhere else.*

I was not too sorry to leave the hut, where no amount of damping down and sweeping up ever made the earthen floor any smoother or cleaner, and where hunger had started to become chronic. We were not overburdened with goods, either, and when we left, without much fuss, on a morning of gleaming light and optimism, there was plenty of room in the wagon behind old Jess for our few pots and pans, the axe and the shovel and a blanket or two. I sat feeling a little dry of throat and damp of eye, because all changes seem to be sad, even those that can only be for the better, holding in my apron the scones

Mrs Leeming had made for us. For once I felt not quite
the lively woman ready for a laugh and life and adventure,
but was strangely a little queasy, a little unsettled, rather
as if I would like to cry and also be sick, just a little,
over the back of the wagon, as Jess jerked forward and
we were, no turning back now, on the road.

We had left our run a bit late, and half the country
seemed to have had the same idea of escaping hunger
by taking to the road, and there was nowhere we came
to where things were any better than what we had left
behind. There were too many gaunt men tramping along
the track who could swing an axe as well as Ken, and
whose bewilderment at what was happening was hidden
behind thick beards, and whose mouths had gone thin
and bitter: and in any case the lucky folk who could call
a bit of land their own were not doing well enough to
pay another man to do their chopping for them. Every
bit of hillside or river valley had its selector's hut where
the pair of earth-colored dour people who had settled
there would come to the door or lean on something to
pass the time of day with us, but they had nothing to
offer us, and had almost as little as we did ourselves.

Being travellers for the duration—and we could not
know how long it might take for us to find our promised
land—I made a pretence to myself for the longest time
that it was the travelling upsetting me, the jolting, the
uncertainty. And Ken made me fans from cabbage palm,
and let me be reckless with the water in the water bag,
wetting a rag for me and handing it to me to wipe my
yellow face. Ken was a good and kindly man, his hard
hands the greatest comfort to me under the stars at night,
but he was as obtuse as I was trying to be, and finally
had to be told in blank words, I could not think of any
fancy ones, and anyway on a damp night of over-generous
dew under our bit of stretched canvas it was not the

225

time or place to be fancy. *Ken, love, I am in the family way,* I said into the dark, imagining the words floating out of my mouth and into the air like a smell, coming in at his earholes to be sniffed at. He lay for so long in silence I wondered if I had really spoken, and whether I should say it again, that speech that I had rehearsed so often in the last few days that the words had no meaning any more for me. It had been an effort to make the words come the first time, but I took breath to say them again: *Ken, love,* I began, but he began to speak at the same moment: *Joanie, love,* he said in a voice dark with feeling, *You are a little beauty.*

I was filled with joy that Ken was glad, but it was all hard going, and I knew that things would be harder before they were easier. How I envied those skinny selectors now! They might have had no more in the way of goods than we did, but they were at least able to stay put in the one spot, and become familiar with the shapes of their own trees and hills.

We would pull up outside one of those huts and Jess would drop her tired head and nuzzle the dust while Ken and I got down stiffly: then the man would stand with Ken, kicking, both of them, at a bit of dirt in front of their boots and exchanging a rumble of words now and again to punctuate the silence. The woman and I would stand by her door or in her sad makeshift hut, and she would be soft with me and my huge belly, and a silence would fall that was pity on her part. I would imagine how later she would say to her husband *What a terrible shocking thing, that poor unfortunate wretch, on the road behind a horse, with only a few pots and pans and a bit of canvas overhead at night, and the baby due any minute.*

The kindest ones urged me to stay, urged me to persuade Ken to tie up the horse next to theirs for a few weeks until the child was safely born. *It could come in the middle of the night, and no one near,* they would say, those too dim to think that I might not have thought of that myself. Those I would have loved to stay with until my time came, the older, fatter ones with a squalling and scampering brood of their own and comfortable hands and eyes: they did not need to put my fears into words for me, but looked into my face and saw them there, the fears and the great weariness.

As my time grew closer my fear grew so great I could not blot it out of my mind, for I knew so little of what I must expect, only that it would be a pain that would make me scream and groan, and that it might go on and on, and that I might die like that, clenched over something unbearable, or with my red life seeping away unstoppably between my legs.

God was on my side, though, holding me in his hand in spite of all my private abuse of Him from time to time, for making life such a hard road. He provided me, at the last moment, when I knew my pains were about to start, with a short stout woman whose voice could have cut through ironbark, but with fat competent hands full of compassion, and knowing brown eyes full of kindness. She asked me nothing and suggested nothing, only looked hard into my face and pushed me into the hut and made me lie on the sacking bed, and felt my gross belly with her squat shrewd hands. She palped and smiled at me at last from her brown eyes that got lost in her cheeks when she smiled, and said in that voice that could have brought the cows in from five miles out: *Well, you have a good big babe there, love, and it is ready and waiting to come and join us all.*

At the door, black shapes against the sunlight, her own children peered and jostled and whispered sibilantly to each other, and without turning or taking her hands off my belly she said, *Youse kids will get the strap if youse*

227

don't make yourselves scarce now. The doorway stood
square and blank again and she looked into my face and
winked, so I could have wept with the relief of being
under the hands of this woman who knew so well how
to manage. *It is your first, love, am I right?* she asked,
and hardly needed to see me nod, because this was a
woman who knew what was what.

Then she got up from where she had been squatting
on the dirt floor beside the bed, pushed herself up with
her stubby hands on her knees with a grunt, and went
quickly to the door. I got up, more slowly, because I
enjoyed lying on a bed once more, even this bed that
was just a bit of bag stretched over a few saplings, but
I made myself get up too and face the glaring sun outside
and the silent hanging trees. *Bob,* she called across the
clearing to where the men were kicking away at a bit of
fencepost and swapping their few phrases, *Bob,* she called
out of her stout little chest, *these two are gunna be
stopping here till the babe comes.* Her husband just nodded
once, then again, and turned away back to Ken, who
stood beside him looking like no one more important
than another man taking refuge behind his whiskers and
brown hat. I watched Ken with love, unworried for once
under the wing of this stout woman, and I knew he was
much more than just another wordless kicking man, and
safe now in competent hands I loved him all over again.

I had not known what to expect—what woman can?
and was in such a blur of being heavy and thick of mind
as well as body that in the end I could not even seem
to summon fear. At the first pang I had cried aloud *No!
I am not ready yet!* but the event was ready for me,
whether or not I was ready for it. Then the pains began:
at first almost something droll, the way they were so
punctual, like a man with a dog walking past your front
gate every five minutes exactly: it was such a clockwork

thing in the beginning it was difficult to take it seriously. But of course the clock began to run faster and faster, so there was no time to laugh at the man with the dog before oh, there he was again, and there he was, and there he was, and there he was, and what had been in the beginning an experimental sort of hand clenching a handful of tissue in my belly became a giant's fist wrenching and clenching and then letting go, but coming again to grip and grasp and twist. At the start it was enough to take a deep breath and think of blue sky above a gum tree and a kookaburra laughing among leaves, but as the grip of the hand grew fiercer and quicker those deep breaths grew jumpy, they were a sort of hard-forced jerky laugh, or was it a cry, and my mind clutched at anything, but everything slid away—Matthew Mark Luke and John, Humpty Dumpty, Oh God Our Help in Ages Past—and all that was left in my head was one two three four five six seven: numbers, which I had always disliked for being such straight-up-and-down things, came to me and chanted themselves through my brain until, in extremity, among groans so loud they made me hoarse, my daughter was born into the short fat hands of Amy.

Afterwards we all knew we could not stay, even though I had come to love Amy as I had never loved any woman, and could have lived forever by her side shelling peas together into a tin dish or plunging our hands into flour. Tears ran shining out of her brown eyes, and she gave up wiping them away with the corner of her pinny, but let them flow, so that the two youngest clutched at her skirt and stared up into her face with their grubby fat faces creased with worry. They plucked with their small hands, wordless with anxiety in the face of some large event that was happening to that solid mother they knew, that dense and dependable small body that knew everything. As I would perhaps have many more sad farewells,

bumping off down a track and seeing a loved face become
nothing with distance, so these children were furrowing
their faces with the first of many puzzling griefs.

*You will come back, love, and give us a look at her
when she is up a bit,* Amy shouted—even in grief her
voice could have led an army—and I nodded, *Yes, we
will come for a visit, and I promise she will remember
you, Amy, she will never forget what you did for her.* We
both knew that this was so much balderdash, Ken and
I would never return this way, and our daughter would
never again see the woman who had saved us both and
delivered us into the world. But I would always remember
Amy, and the best I could hope for would be some pale
woman jolting down a bit of track that Ken and I would
call our own someday, and me going out to help her
down off the wagon and give her a bed and what help
I could, until she too had to set off again into some dusty
future. I could only hope to repay Amy like that, and
meet her again disguised as some other poor wretch of
a human in distress.

I clung to that vision of a future, with solid ground
under me and some kind of roof over my head, as I
clung to the baby over a thousand bumps and stumps
and ruts, through days that passed in a blur of all that
was awful, with fatigue like chains around me. It was
with mixed feelings that I heard Ken say we had almost
left the last of the selectors' huts behind. That meant an
end even to what little feeling of safety I had had, the
feeling that when tiny Lucy looked yellow, or blazed hot
under my hand, down the track there might possibly be
some version of Amy, who could tell me that it was
nothing to worry over, or that a bit of camphor on a
hot rag would fix it in no time.

But now the track was almost no longer there and Ken
spent most of his days up ahead with the horse, leading

her by the nose around trees and stones and leaving us in the droning heat of midday to go ahead, looking for a drop of water in some muddy waterhole and a route through the trees that the wagon might manage. At dusk he would come back and stretch our canvas over a sapling or a rope, light a fire and get the billy going while I lay too weary even to watch, with Lucy, weary too after the head of the day and a tiring tug on my nipples, fingering my breasts and sighing like a sad old woman. I watched Ken, and knew I loved him all the more for the way he had grown even more silent, worrying over his wife and daughter and wearying himself day after day with this heartless prickly bush country. I knew I loved him, but was too stunned even to feel such a thing as love, almost too weary even to make the blood continue to flow, however sluggishly, along my veins.

There were times when I remembered myself as a skinny girl, declaring to the chooks at dawn that I would not end up like my bedraggled mother, or any of those other wornout women I saw around me. Even the chooks had been scrawny, their feathers dirty and hopeless, their silly eyes lackluster, their scratchings at the beaten earth feeble. The rooster had preened and primped, having only his cockadoodling to worry about, not the laying and hidden lurking of eggs on his mind. I had no wish to be that silly puffed-up rooster strutting his idiocy on a pile of smelly cabbage leaves, but I had sworn as I flung wheat at those sad chooks that I would keep myself lithe, young, elastic of flesh and mind, always sufficient to myself, and not bowed down with a squalling brood or a dour husband.

Ah, I had sworn and grown hot with the conviction that I was special, but now I lay under a tree, trying to pretend I was comfortable enough in spite of a bit of tree root sticking into my spine, because I was too tired to move. Here I was—not lithe, not elastic, and not myself any longer, but hostess to tiny demanding Lucy, and the prisoner of my love for her. And for Ken, too, as dour and sour-sweated a man as any man could be, with the few words coming out from between his lips as if they cost the earth, but I was held prisoner by my love for him, too, for the way his eyes spoke to mine when we woke together on our blanket, and he was tender as he pushed back the hair at my temple and stroked my cheek, in those few minutes we were allowed before another endless day of sun and jolting and flies began.

It was our last day on the road when we met Fred— Fred McCubbin of course—although we did not know then that our time in the wilderness was nearly over. I lay in the blessed cool and dimness of dusk, under a tree, flat on my back with Lucy asleep and dribbling into my stomach, watching the blue smoke of Ken's little fire drift through the trees and lie like water under the branches. I watched Ken and wondered if I would manage another day of this distress, but knew I had no choice, and whispered aloud to myself, so that Lucy shuffled and snuffled: *It will not go on forever.* I saw Ken straighten up from the fire, the billy in his hand, and stare towards me, so I wondered if I had not been whispering at all but shouting at the top of my tired lungs. But now Ken was putting the billy down again and turning with both hands empty, staring, I could see now, not at me, but past me down the bit of track where we had come.

Anyone could see even at this distance that Fred was no hungry swaggie with the soles out of his shoes. Something in the cut of his swag and the way his hat sat on his head, something a bit stooped, was it, about the shoulders, as if he crouched over books more than he swung at ironbark with an axe, and something a bit finicky about the way he put his feet down, made me

232

watch as Ken was doing and forget the tiredness in the curiosity of watching him.

We stared at Fred, and he slowed and stared at us too, in a bright pleased way that was not the usual way folk on the track greeted each other. He slowed and finally stood watching, as if memorizing every detail of the way I lay under the tree with Lucy, and the way Ken was still half-bent over the fire, and the way the smoke was drifting along the ground. He smiled a smile full of confident white teeth, a bit of a city smile, I thought, for bush folk do not do too much smiling, especially not at strangers, and not at the end of a long day on the track.

He stared, and called out at last: *You make a picture, the three of you there, good enough to hang in a frame, the three of you on the wallaby track.*

JOAN

AGAIN I came to know dawns, this time wakened by tiny tyrannical cries, when grubby light washed into the sky, or when blazes of scarlet and gold made everything look like a gaudy unconvincing painting. I would sit in the old brown armchair, feeling tiny Madge nibble away busily at a nipple, her eyes closed with concentration, her lips tucked tight around my flesh. I would sit there, slack in the chair, watching the light strengthen on the white walls of the room and turn from pink to white, and see outside how the sky shifted from pearly shades of grey and luminous no-color to the palest, cleanest of blues. The dawn dance the sky performed every morning was its moment of greatest glory, but who was there to applaud? A few weary mothers dizzy with longing for sleep, and a few trudging early workers at shifts in various laborious trades, the lucky ones still warm from the egg and bacon made for them by some loving soul at home, but most plodding along living on the hope of some better tomorrow, with the flat taste of futility in their mouths. And, I supposed, a few of that other dawn variety of person: the silent-footed shadowy swift kind, with a few small tools in a cloth bag and a skilful way with a

237

window in its frame, and light fingers with trinkets of value.

These dawns, like those others in the creaking wicker chair in the desert, brought tears to my eyes, but this time not the stinging tears of rage and ennui. What were these tears? It seemed to me as the days passed that I was weeping for everyone: I wept for the mothers of sick infants, bending low over them in their feverish cots, willing health back to their limp bodies: I wept for women who did not have the luxury of a chair, and a breast full of good warm milk, but had to squat—I had seen the pictures—on a bit of parched dusty earth, with their few rags fluttering in the desert wind, gaunt with anguish as their skinny babies, too weak to cry their hunger, sucked hopelessly, wearily, at an empty breast. I wept for the fathers watching their wives and children subside into heaps of bony limbs and rags, never to rise again: I wept for the misery and injustice of it all, and wept my thanks that Madge lay, fat-limbed, content, snuffling and gulping into a breast running over with what she needed.

I wept for myself, too, of course: wept with relief that, fool though I had been, and hard of heart, callous and obdurate as a stone, I had still been forgiven by Duncan and by life, which was now filling its cup to the brim for me. Here I was, totally necessary to tiny Madge, whose life was at this moment nothing, if it was not a milky breast, and then a shoulder to burp on: and I was necessary to Duncan too, in a small way, although Duncan would never again allow any person to become too necessary to him.

I too had become a person of needs, had given over my life and happiness into the hands of others in a way that would have made me shudder, or laugh in scorn in my ruthless younger days. Tiny Madge was necessary to me now, so much so that, parted from her for an hour,

I felt my being stretched out to her, joined as if by an elastic thread that tugged and tweaked, making me distracted, like someone with toothache or a tight shoe, until I was with her again. Then there was Duncan: I knew now, as never before, how necessary he was to me, and made myself groan at night sometimes, imagining the bed without his warmth beside me, and the bleakness of dawn in a house without him.

I had been lucky: I had had choices not open to most women. I had taken on the sex of the ones who make history: I had become a man, and I had seen, in time, that that was not what I wanted. I had thought that to make history one had to be a man, or at least to achieve something large and visible. History, I had thought, was a mountain discovered and named, or a battle won, or a nation led to greatness.

Now I could see that this was an unpleasant trick at the expense of the world's majorities, who would never do any such things as those. All the nameless men of the world who labored with shovels, and even more all the nameless women of the world, bending over babies and cooking-fires, were also part of history. They had been unfairly excluded from the glory, and taught that they were of no account: they had been taught to despise what they spent their lives doing, and to dismiss it as insignificant, not worthy of anyone's time or a place in the books. But without those nameless multitudes, where would the heroes be? If there had been no one to wash their socks, bring up their children, and peel their potatoes, what would they have been able to achieve? Nothing. No mountains could have been discovered, no atoms harnessed, no armies led to victory. No, I saw that although I had chosen to be that most invisible of creatures, the wife and mother, I had chosen the destiny where history was most truly to be made: mine was the history not of an individual, but of the whole tribe of humanity keeping the generations flowing along.

I saw in that armchair with the bulging springs, with long pale stains where Madge had burped too enthusiastically, and wept for the past and the present, and for the future as well. I sat with Madge's sweet warmth and weight in the crook of my arm and her feet bumping out her bliss against my leg, her fingers grasping at my breast, fingering the flesh as if to learn it by heart. I sat and saw our futures together, our futures which from this moment, where we were flesh of one flesh, would be a gradual process of separation.

JOAN MAKES HISTORY

SCENE ELEVEN

In 1901 Australia ceased to be a colony of Britain
and became a self-governing nation. When the first
parliament was opened that year by the heir to the
throne, I, Joan, participated in that occasion of
splendor.

I was resplendent, comparatively, in the black charmeuse
with the purple embroidered lisse jabot. To tell you
the truth, I fancied myself at least as fine as any of these
other women, although it had been a great disappointment
not to be able to wear the peacock-blue mousseline-de-
soie that did such a lot for me: but everyone was looking
sallow in black for our dear departed Sovereign, so we
were all in the same boat, and I was sure I was grand
enough for the occasion, and for my position. After all,
I was the wife of the Mayor of Castleton, a mother of
six, and grandmother of three, and none of that was to
be sneezed at.

True, George and I had not arrived in our own carriage
for the occasion of the Opening of Parliament, but in
the hackney from Foyle's. I supposed too, that some of
these peau-de-soies and crêpe-de-chines in the throng had
cost more than my charmeuse, and some of them had
no doubt been constructed in Paris or London by su-
percilious women who snapped their fingers and made
minions run with pins. In spite of that, I swelled with
pride within my purple embroidered lisse jabot, knowing
that I was as good as any of those other pigeon busts. I
had no doubt that some of theirs, like mine, were cun-

ningly padded with horsehair and pongee to make up for
what Nature had seen fit to be niggardly about.

The Exhibition Building was resplendent, too, with
bunting and flags snapping and heaving against a breeze,
and the trees of the grounds bowing and curtseying to
each other as the fine gentlefolk were doing, milling on
the paths. Behind the barricades, people in cloth caps
pointed and stared and fat women in calico aprons held
babies up to see history being made. There was a family
of black folk there too, clustered together and watching
without any kind of expression at all: but no one liked
to give too much thought to them and what they might
be thinking.

Carriage after carriage drew up and everyone craned
to see who it was, and if it was someone whom everyone
knew, such as Lord and Lady Tennyson, or dear Nellie
Melba herself (what a cheer went up when she stepped
out, and a hush fell as if we half-expected her to open
her mouth then and there and let her voice soar out), a
pleased bright murmur went through both crowds, the
silk one and the calico one, for everyone likes to recognize
the famous.

At the start of the day, I had congratulated myself for
being a member of this nation, and I felt that it was
truly the way they said it was, that this was a land of
equality and justice for all, an example to the bad old
lands with histories too long ever to be put right. It must
be so, for here were George and I, folk from humble
origins, up here rubbing shoulders with the highest in
the land.

After all, I had grown up in a hut with a dirt floor
and had shared a pair of boots with my sister, so we
could never go into town at the same time: I had worn
smocks made of flour bags and had filled up with plenty
of damper and dripping in my time. And when George

and I had married, and he had started up the business, we had had to count every penny. I had made the sheets of the cheapest unbleached calico, and made them last by turning sides to middle, and had spent my evenings darning George's socks and turning his collars, and patching the children's clothes and running string along the inside of hems for when they needed letting down: I had grated up carrot to make cakes stick together when eggs had been scarce, and knew how to make scrag end into a good meal. And now, when we had arrived by such hard work and thrift at a position of comfort, here I was, creaking in the best whalebone, sweating discreetly in my charmeuse, up here with the grandest.

George and I were not altogether comfortable among such fine clothes and genteel speech, such display and waste, but I knew we would not disgrace ourselves today, for we had learned, laboriously, what these grand folk had been born to and could do without giving it a thought.

We had not taken in etiquette with our mother's milk, and there were still small issues on which I had to keep my eyes open and see how others did it, and I still had to make discreet enquiries of folk I trusted, and had a small collection of books hidden away on the subject of manners in the best society. And for this day in particular I had prepared with the greatest care, because there would never again be a day like this one, and what if I should be presented to Nellie Melba or Lady Tennyson, and need to know how to address her? Should she be *Ma'am*, or *My Lady*, or *Your Ladyship*, or what should she be? The book was tantalizing on this subject: *A knight's wife, is, of course, Lady Blank*, it told me smugly, *and is never addressed by her equals as Your Ladyship*. Not being an equal, that did not help me much, but I thought I would be safe with *Ma'am*: or would that make me sound like a servant girl? And what if I was (or *were*, as I tried to remember to say), confronted with the problem of an introduction: *Mrs X, may I present Mr Y?* And what of the controversy surrounding the curtsey, which some said was quite out of fashion, while others were adamant that it was still quite the thing, or *de rigueur,* as I had read but never dared to say? Even the handshake was a matter of anxiety: I had taken to heart the importance of avoiding the *flabby palm,* the *crushing grasp,* and the *clinging clasp,* until I felt as stiff about it all as a plank.

I had practiced eating asparagus with the fingers, had studied lists of who—or was it whom?—should precede who through doorways, and had become deft in fan-manipulation: I had rehearsed in the cheval glass various expressions and movements, and the kind of elegantly long-winded ways of saying it was a fine day that were essential in good society. Preparedness had always been my forte: I had always carried a supply of safety pins and sal volatile in my reticule as a mark of my preparedness, and I was sure I had thought of everything for this day. I had even rehearsed the controversial curtsey, in case I should come face to face, somehow, with the Duke and Duchess themselves: I knew I would feel it *de rigueur* to curtsey then, whatever the fashionable said, and I had made little Alice squeal with the fun of seeing Gran practice, spreading my skirts in a deep teetering curtsey.

I had consulted with George on my only doubt: the propriety of taking opera glasses along. Would that be a mark of the proper enthusiasm, or would it be merely vulgar? The books were strangely silent on this matter, and George had submerged into a great deal of silent frowning thought, during which he fingered his watch chain in the way I knew so well, and loved for knowing that it meant serious thought and self-doubt: at last he said in his most mayoral tones, somewhat adenoidal in their seriousness: *Yes, that would seem an appropriate thing, Joanie, although in moderation.*

I had prepared so hard that I found myself purblind and half deaf on arrival at the building glittering and twinkling in the sun: so much finery and so many important men and their swaybacked wives! Everywhere I looked in the throng, I saw faces I knew from the illustrated papers, and I succumbed to a kind of daze in which the only solid thing was George's arm, keeping me upright and dignified.

I tried, though, to collect myself and take note, because Alice, that newest and best-loved of all our grandchildren, had demanded that I tell her every detail: to tell her *everything, Gran, every single thing, promise.* And it was no hardship to peer and crane at details of fichus and collarettes, for I had always been inclined to be a bit of a stickybeak, and this was a busybody's treat, peering at everyone around us, slow-moving women cautious with their parasols in the crush, and their menfolk looking cross with the gravity of it all.

I stared and suddenly found myself exclaiming to George: *Why, there is Lady McNab,* and a women next to us turned to stare at me. I was fool enough to feel proud of knowing Lady McNab, and it passed through my ignoble mind to say something that would make the woman know that not only did I recognize Lady McNab, but that I had dined in her company in Castleton, on the occasion of the laying of the foundation stone of the Castleton and District Hospital. George and I had enjoyed a haunch of good meat, and French wine in crystal glasses, and had laughed with everyone else at her husband's laborious tales of Surrey hunts, and at hers of the droll banter at Amblehurst, and I had even sympathized with the way you could not get good help these days, and the way servants were beyond words grand and troublesome.

George and I had sat and smiled, and been seduced by it all, although uneasy.

She is looking better than when we saw her last, I could not resist saying now to George, and he nodded without saying anything, for he had not enjoyed that day or that dinner, and had been made uncomfortable by Lord and Lady. George had too much natural honor to have thought of impressing the stranger in front of us with our intimacy with English aristocracy.

It was no great surprise to see Lady McNab here: she was higher gentry than we, after all. The surprise was that Lady McNab had seen us too, had caught my eye and was making her way towards us to speak. I was somewhat astonished: in such a crush it would have been easy for her to bow slightly and move on, and after all at that fine dinner the Mayor and his wife had been only minor guests, people of no real account: but I was pleased and flattered and proud, for this must truly be a day when *all hearts were joined, regardless of rank, to the same great goal,* as the papers had said that morning, and *all distinction of degree was forgotten.*

Well, Lady McNab advanced on us, huge in gleaming satin that made her look like a gigantic muscatel, and I waited confidently, knowing the right thing to do. I waited with one foot slightly behind the other, preparing to perform my vestigial bob, of which the exact degree of drop was a matter of fine judgment, regulating nicely the exact degree of deference. But even as I was on the point of performing my bob, Lady McNab beamed with all her fine teeth and made a grand gesture with her right hand, a gesture of bestowing, and I had to recognize that she had made a different decision on the matter of curtsies she was offering me her hand to shake.

Frankly I panicked. At war within my horsehair and pongee chest were two imperatives: the one, that a hand proffered from aristocracy was never to be refused: the other, that a lady never shakes hands with her gloves on. Now, I am not a woman of pretension, and know I am no lady, and can only excuse myself by saying that in my panic there seemed only one possible thing to do. In the few seconds left to me while Lady McNab's hand was outstretched, I must remove, with all haste and decorum, the glove from my right hand.

It was panic, of course, or I would never have been so mad as to imagine all those tiny mother-of-pearl buttons could possibly be undone in time. It was panic, and I felt the raw blood bursting in my veins, engorging into a blush over my whole body, so the glove seemed to become part of my flesh, never to be removed in time for contact with the palm of Lady McNab. It was panic, and there was no time, and finally what those warring imperatives left me with was a glove only half-removed from the hand, so that it was empty fingers of black suede kid that were shaken by Lady McNab. Lady McNab, that smiling gracious grape, smiled all the more and seemed to linger endlessly over the business of shaking the hand, or the glove, of the lady wife of the Mayor of Castleton. I knew that many a marvellous Melbourne dinner party would rock with laughter, such as would alarm the maids sedate by their sideboards, as she told this story of a jumped-up shopkeeper's wife who thought she was as good as quality.

I was still swollen with the mortification of this when men in livery began to herd us to our allotted places. We all moved with a great silken rustling into the great hall, under the mighty arches and domes. At least there I could bow my blazing face down into my chest and try, in the change of place, to put behind me that grotesque moment of ill-judged etiquette, although even when we were shown to our places I was still hot and was starting

249

to wish the day was over. We had been allotted a place in one of the high galleries, a long way up, and as far away from the dais as it was possible to be while still being actually in the hall, so that I was glad of my opera glasses: here it was easy to see a quite precise gradation of rank, from the most grand down close to the Prince, to the most humble up here, where the heat gathered in a smell of feet and we were packed in rather tightly together.

For Alice's sake, I stared and strained with the rest to catch sight of the heir apparent to the throne. I could see by glimpses a pale puny sort of man, covered in froggings and braid, with bits of colored ribbon on his chest, and most of his face covered with hair. He stood in a great shaft of light from a window high up, a small man with a cocked hat that seemed too large for his head, and read his few words full of bombast, while we all strained to hear over the unceasing shuffle of feet on the wooden floors.

I counted the people on the stage and tried to remember the mousseline-de-soies and the ostrich feathers, the arrangements of bows and curls, and the way the Duchess stood leaning ever so slightly on her watered-silk parasol. Down there on the dais, the important people were doing their best to look solemn, and not to sway where they stood at attention: the men had become all chest, the women rigid under their stays, and the white plumes of the helmets of the men in uniform had gone limp in the heat.

The band blared and we shuffled our programmes: *All People That On Earth Do Dwell,* we sang, the echoes of so many voices blurring the song into a great droning muddle of sound like a melancholy beehive. Then the speeches began, and I did my best to hear what was being said. But up here where the minor folk were situated,

there was little to be heard, just a great breathing, the
sighing of thousands of people present at history, and
from up here the words ebbed and flowed like the sea,
sometimes audible, sometimes not, so that it looked as
though nothing much more important was happening
than a lot of mouths opening and closing, and lips shaping
themselves with hot air around grand phrases.

All those dark mouth-holes were making the history
of their land, and making it in their own image, so that
as far as I could hear, that history was one of pastures
and acquisitions, pounds and acres: it was a history full
of great men, men like themselves with whiskers and
hats that concealed their eyes, and long ponderous sen-
tences that concealed their souls. They spoke of *progress,*
it was a word they seemed fond of, and which they
uttered with enough conviction to bring it all the way
up to us in our distant gallery. A few other words were
robust enough to last the distance: words such as *enterprise* and *initiative,* and under these splendid words were
others that no one quite uttered, but which we could all
hear just the same: these unspoken words were ones like
cash and *profit,* and the images were of gold things, of
wads of banknotes, of fawning bankers, of diamonds
against skin, of minions pandering. It was men in the
leather armchairs of clubs admiring other men for making
more *cash* and *profit:* it was tight-skinned pert children
going to the best schools and having great things expected
of them: it was an image of beating the other fellow,
squeezing another few pounds out of a deal or labor out
of a minion, or objects out of a heap of some raw material:
it was pride in being sharp, and pleasure in paying some
ferret-nosed gent to find a way of breaking the laws
without the laws being able to do anything: it was riding
along in a fine carriage and seeing men in caps look up
as they trudged, or lined up in front of the Works at

Christmas, cheering on a signal from the foreman and being grateful for their Christmas boxes. Above all it was the satisfaction of having more than nearly everyone else, and the feeling that they deserved it all, for having also been cleverer than nearly everyone else.

My encounter with Lady McNab had punctured my pride somewhat, and I had been reminded all too brutally that I was not, in spite of my elegant charmeuse and the books about asparagus, on the same level as Lady McNab and her like. I was piqued and punctured, and as I stood growing weary of distant words, I found an argumentative frame of mind coming on. *What of the others, the ones who are not in this hall?* I became indignant and wanted to ask: *What of those who lived here before us? What of all the people who will melt away like mud when they die, remembered in no book of history?*

However, I had no cause for complacency: it was true that George and I were not in the business of stripping this land of all it had, and wringing profit out of every transaction, and we did not think it clever to do a man out of a living wage: but here we were, standing stiff in our best, listening to such men as if we admired them: we were accomplices. We were happy enough to be Mayor and wife of Mayor: we stood, fleshy ourselves, listening to other fleshy folk speak of *opportunity* and *freedom,* when we knew it meant their own opportunity, their own freedom, to do nothing but make profit on profit and let the rest go hang.

Finally the last speech, prayer, hymn, and blessing had gone floating up on its puff of hot air: the Duke had said his piece, and had pressed the button for the flags to be raised all over Australia, and we had all cheered and clapped until we did not quite know how to stop. Then the band put an end to it, blaring out a sort of march to get us on the move, and there was a hubbub of people pleased with themselves for having witnessed history, and glad it was over, so that they could find a place for a bit of a sitdown.

The books would have many a fine phrase for what we had seen: they would tell how the hearts of all had *swelled with tumultuous feeling,* how the Duke had stood in a beam of light as if *illumined by the Finger of God:* how the *thunderstorm of cheering* had shaken the building to its foundations, and how we had emerged into the *dawn of a new age of liberty and hope.*

In fact, George and I emerged into a din that made my ears ring, of people shouting and exclaiming: close by us on the steps two men boomed a lot of laughter out of their chests, and a woman called shrilly *Come ON, Percy, for heaven's sake!* and was drowned out by cheering from some group I could not see, over to the side. There was a din from the crowd beyond the barricades, of wooden rattles being whirled, and whistles blown: babies wailed, dogs barked, horses and carriages clattered on the road: I was made dizzy by the battery of noise, and by so much feeling running high.

I knew I should be wanting to join the exultation, but I could not find it in me to rejoice: I felt surly about it all now, and the more these other people believed in it, the more aloof I was. *It is all just so many fine words,* I called, made a little hysterical by the clamor. *Just words!* I heard my voice go shrill and strange, but in the din no one seemed to hear: a man in a topper next to us turned and seemed to stare at me, but then he waved and smiled and nodded at someone over my shoulder: even he had not heard. *Joanie, Joanie,* I heard George beside me, and felt him squeeze my hand: he at least had heard, but it was not George whom I wanted to make listen, but those others. *Do not believe them!* I shouted, or tried to, but I could hear how reedy, how thin, how puny my voice was, how the words were lost as soon as they left my lips, and all at once I was consumed with tears.

I recovered myself on the steps at the side of the crowd, sitting hiccupping and gulping while George fanned me with his programme and warded off a fat woman thrusting smelling salts into my face. *It is just the excitement,* George mumbled at her. *Just a short spell and she will be right.* The fat woman left and gradually the clamor died away. The rattles stopped one by one, or grew more distant as the crowd wandered away along the paths: boys got sick of blowing their whistles, everyone ran out of laughing and things to shout to each other, and the minds of most began to turn toward lunch. George and I sat on our step while the carriages all rolled away bearing the gentry off to their silver and damask, and the men in cloth caps and the women in aprons straggled back along the avenues, their babies asleep over their shoulders, looking forward to a plate of cold mutton and a glass of stout. Now we could hear the wind in the trees and a bird or two: we could hear doors slamming behind us in the hollow building where it had happened, and a broom somewhere close at hand sweeping a path, and a pail of water being set down with a clank.

George stood up and I stood too, and took his hand. He tucked it up against him: I felt foolish and flat now, and there seemed nothing to have become so excited about. The bunting looked ragged, the grass was ugly and trampled where the barricades had been, and all the glory had evaporated from the scene. Everyone had gone, even the group of blacks was nowhere to be seen, unless a cluster of shadows under a distant tree might have been them. *It is silly,* I whispered, meaning myself as well as the pomp we had seen, but George squeezed my hand tighter. *But we were here, Joanie, and saw it with our own eyes,* he said. *We were on the spot.*

We did not say any more about my lapse, but walked in an agreeable silence along the avenues of trees. *Alice will nag us for every blessed thing,* I said at last, and George smiled and said, *By Jove, we had better not leave anything out or there will be strife!* We walked along smiling then, for Alice was at the age of questions, and we both knew the way she would pluck at my skirt and insist: *Then what, Gran, what happened then?*

What had happened? Well, some grand men had said some grand words, and those inclined that way had got a bit dewy of eye about it all. Other things had happened too: I would not shirk from telling Alice how my glove had made a fool of me, and how I had thought the Duke looked like an impostor in someone else's hat, and how I had got hot and bothered at the end, and made a spectacle of myself in a small shrill way. It would not matter that we would not be able to tell her the precise words that the Duke had used, or exactly how many notables had been on the dais, or just who they were, for she would be able to read that in any of the books. What we would be able to tell her was priceless, for it was all that no one else could tell her, all the things no book would ever mention. They were peculiar, lopsided, absurd sorts of things that we would tell her: they were things that would look silly in a book, and no one would be tempted to make a bronze statue out of any of them. They mattered just the same, for they were the rest of the history, and without them it was all wrong. *Alice,* I would say seriously, so that she would become solemn and her eyes would grow very big, watching my face for what I would tell her: *Listen carefully now, for this is your inheritance.*

JOAN

HERE is our Madge, caught by the Brownie held by her proud father. She is ten years old, and this is an educational excursion: today Duncan and I, and Madge and her somewhat smug little friend, neat catlike Caroline, and the other friend, gangly slack-jawed Ellen from next door, have all crammed into the creaking black Humber with the peeling walnut-veneer dashboard. Here we all are, standing on an ugly bit of municipal concrete, pointing theatrically at a squat obelisk behind a chain with spikes in it, as if it would be everyone's first thought to make off with this ugly object. It marks the spot where the first British foot stepped ashore at Botany Bay, and the first British flag was raised. Why are we there? *They should see it,* Duncan had said. *We should all see it, Joanie, have you seen it?* And I had to say I had not, and Duncan, too, shook his head over his porridge, for he had not seen it either. *Let us go today then,* he said, and dabbed at a bit of spilled porridge on his knee. *The birthplace of the nation, after all, Joanie, our history started there, in a manner of speaking.*

Neat Caroline has taken up a strategic position to the left of the obelisk, so that she can point tidily to it while still smiling for the Brownie. Her fringe glistens, her ears stick out below her home-made pudding-basin haircut and her pale cardigan hangs neatly by her sides. Her feet are together—oh, what a well-brought-up and obedient little person she is, and how insufferably pleased with herself (the insufferable friends of your children is something no one warns you about). *What does our Madge have to do with her?* Duncan and I ask each other in the murmuring time before sleep, and we have no answers, for our unruly Madge is like chalk to the soapy cheese of smiling Caroline.

On the other side of this puny monument is Ellen, whose features have not quite co-ordinated themselves enough for a smile, let alone a smile of Caroline's relentless kind: poor Ellen's mouth is ajar on one or two of her yellow and crooked teeth—*She'll have the lot out at twenty and be shot of them, like I done,* her mother has shouted to me between the tea towels on the line. Although Ellen means well, her eyes are wandering away at the vital button-clicking instant and she is slumping sideways, propping up on the side of a foot, all crooked lines and awkward contrivances against gravity, like a barn leaning over with all its angles wrong, and a plank holding it up at the back because no one has thought it worthwhile to mend it properly. Ellen lives on potato and bread, and could not care less about obelisks or history, poor thing, caring only about avoiding the strap from her fierce boilermaker's-riveter's-mate of a father (and I have seen that strap, a thick leather belt that hangs out in the laundry), and about not having to exert herself. She is always tired, always listless, always pale with too much bread and jam, always having to be chivvied by Madge (I have eavesdropped, pretending to hang out a sheet or pull a weed) into any game that involves more than sprawling in the shade. But although Duncan and I can tut-tut about her teeth, the strap, all that bread,

260

there is no need to ask why our mercurial Madge should be with such a slow-coach—Ellen is the girl next door, and even the most sluggish of playmates is better than none at all.

And our Madge, where is she? There she is, between her friends, directly in front of the podgy obelisk, so she is caught wondering how to go about pointing at it. One foot is beginning to turn towards it, a hand is beginning an awkward gesture over a shoulder, and her face is full of the mischief of someone spoiling the snap for her serious father, frowning into the tiny square of life caught in the glass of the viewfinder.

That father, my Duncan, was becoming bored now with these tidy walks and wallows of dirty water. I watched him slip the strap of the Brownie over his hand and push back his sleeve in an ostentatious way, checking the time, and then stare off over the dunes where the black folk lived, so that no one would involve him in a conversation that would delay our going.

The girls were arguing now: they knew, even dull Ellen knew, that the obelisk had not been here when that first commander had unfurled a mildewed Union Jack, but what of the path, the sea wall, the lawn? Tidy Caroline had no conception of a place without such amenities, and was becoming pink and outraged at Madge's suggestion that there had been just dirt.

What plodding municipal foot was it, activated by what earnest brain, that had decided that this was the very spot, this and no other, on which that first buckled foot had stepped? Someone had pointed and said *Here* with more confidence than was possible, for who could know? Someone had driven in a surveyor's stake, and there the obelisk had been erected, along with a bit of sea wall, nicely made by council workers who had all day to get the curve on the stone just right.

Great moments in history! Here is another: here is our Madge, cross that day because I have made her wear the pink gingham she hates, scowling at her father behind the Brownie, her head down in the sunlight so her eyes are black sockets and her mouth a sulky shadow. She is supposed to be pretending to be Captain Cook, standing in the doorway of his cottage in the middle of the Melbourne greenery, but she is resisting the coaxing of her parents and is standing there mulishly.

But she had been intrigued by that small bleak house with the bare thick planks on the floor and the tiny uncurtained windows: it was a house like a whitewashed box. It was not possible to imagine anyone curling up in those hard-looking cold-looking beds, much less (the look Duncan and I exchanged above Madge's head agreed on this) to imagine Mr and Mrs Cook writhing in passion on that matrimonial bed in its alcove: were folk so much smaller then, or simply used to taking up less space? Duncan and I, our glance agreed, would not have been able to manage in such a tight space, under such a frosty starched counterpane, on such a lumpy and unforgiving mattress.

The tiny cupboard which was the other bedroom, where Mr and Mrs Cook's Madge, if they had had one, would have have lain on her skinny bed, with no space for anything else in the room except for a candle in a pewter holder, was on the other side of a wall that looked like a flimsy and sound-conducting affair.

Madge made a shrill sound of indignation at the sight of the tiny other bedroom: *But there is no room!* she shouted, *why are they so small?* and at last announced in a voice that could have been heard in every corner of this house: *Gee, but I am glad I was not them!* We let our Madge run ahead of us down the tight steep staircase, calling back up impatiently, *Come on! Come*

262

on! but Duncan took a moment to press me into the corner of the staircase and give me a kiss like a small instalment, a down payment, a sample demonstration, of the kind of thing that cheerless bedroom had made us think of.

Now, this one is better altogether. Madge is looking full into the camera, with some sort of a smile on her face, but I can tell you why the smile is crooked, embarrassed, unsure: why her look at the camera, although not cross, is puzzled, diffident, ambiguous. Let me draw your attention to the fact that she, and of course Duncan too, is at a beach. You can see sand and rocks, dune grass and the edge of a shrub and a bit of the lagoon behind the beach, and although the snapshot is grainy black, grainy white, and shades of grainy grey, I can see the way the sand dazzles yellow, can see the grey-green sheen of the dune grass and the shrubs. I can feel the salt breeze and hear the surf behind the camera. We were all there that day, Duncan and Madge and I (I was in the thick black swimsuit I felt appropriate for a middle-aged wife and mother, Duncan in the blue trunks with small red clocks on them, like socks, that I had bought him in a sale somewhere, thrifty housewife that I was), and Madge had befriended some little boy with smooth brown skin and a short fur of hair, who was there in the photo too, holding the stick that was the spear of some game of Aborigines they had been playing.

Well, Madge was wearing her old blue-and-green swimsuit, that was nearly too small for her growing body, so she had become impatient at the way it restricted her shoulders, and had rolled it down to her waist so her flat little-girl chest was exposed. While it was all right to expose her chest to this beach, and to her Mum and Dad, and even to this smooth little boy with sand on his cheek, it seemed to her not all right to expose her nipples to the unblinking eye of the camera. *No,* she had cried, *No, Dad!* as Duncan had stepped back and frowned into the camera, and the boy had stood up straight like a soldier about to be shot.

Duncan fiddled and peered, turned things and peered again, paced out the distance between Madge and himself, and squinted up at the sun, lost in calculations. Madge tried to hoist at the blue-and-green straps, but the whole thing clung to her waist so she could not drag the fabric up, and now Duncan was half-squatting to get the right angle, and started to call out: *Smile now! Smile, kids! This way!* and Madge was appealing to me: *But Mum, my cossie!* for she was not old enough to have any flesh on her chest, and not old enough to know why such inflammatory flesh was covered up, but she was old enough to know that while boys such as this brown one could stand with their flat pink nipples exposed to the camera, the equally flat pink nipples of girls were generally hidden. *But Mum!* she was protesting, bewildered, unsure. *No, Madge, it is okay,* I called, *it does not matter, it is all right, Madge love,* because to me it was absurd and sad that a tiny flat-chested girl had been made ashamed of her bare skin, that her young face should be creasing with uncertainity, that she was not sure whether to be embarrassed, so that even as her father finally clicked the button, she was beginning that sad ashamed gesture of covering her innocent chest with her arms, and looking congested with doubt and shame.

The moment after the snap was taken, I could remember, she had burst into furious tears, and the smug little boy had stared, and his loud-voiced mother had said *Overtired, is she?* so that Madge roared all the louder, and the sun suddenly slid behind the trees, and the sand was all at once cold and nasty, and a breeze was whipping up the waves of Providence Bay as they raced up the steep beach. The day began to trail away into a wearisome hike back to the Humber with the picnic things, and a long cranky drive back home with the thousands of other Humbers, with a picture of our daughter's fall from innocence waiting to emerge from the small black box.

There was no Garden of Eden, ever, for any of us, although here is Madge standing proudly beside a wooden box in which she has planted tops cut from carrots, which are waving in a cheery feathery way, and her bright hopeful face says that she is sure the carrot tops are growing downward, growing another carrot from the stump of the old in the way lizards can grow new tails: that was another small expulsion from childhood's Eden, when at last those feathery leaves grew coarse, yellow, then brown, sent out a feeble flower head or two, then withered away entirely, and oh, we could not look at our Madge's face, crestfallen, all the brightness gone from it, when she dug up the hairy stumps of buried carrot. Even Duncan, keen though he was to immortalize every moment of history, even he knew better than to get out his brand-new camera then and ask poor Madge to pose with the trowel in her hand.

Often I watched from behind an oleander feeling my heart beat like a person watching her love: there was my Madge, a large-faced girl in blue box pleats. She was an active child, and even when smug Caroline and feeble Ellen were nowhere to be found, to be harassed into some game that involved shrieking up and down the garden, and doing things with long sticks, or throwing things (I watched, proud prying mother that I was, and saw that our Madge could always throw further, hurl her stones straighter, run faster, shriek shriller), our Madge could invent her own playmates and her own busy activities. She might spend the morning smearing mud on leaves for sandwiches and baking mud pies, and decorating a

big cake of mud with a peppering of sand in the shape
of a house. Or she might beg me to fill up the old copper
that sat in state in its tumbledown shed, with the black
lines of smoke running up the whitewashed wall behind
it. She would stand in there, stamping at the water,
pretending to be a wine treader, or would find the old
bleached copper-stick, worn to shredded fibres at one end
and shiny on the other from the grasp of who knows
how many washerwomen's hands, and stir a witches'
brew in her cauldron.

Our Madge loved a gun as much as any boy and would
always rather be an Indian than a cowboy. *Bags be Chief
Sitting Bull,* I would hear her shriek from the garden,
and she would come in later, faced darkened with dirt,
boasting about how good she was at dying. *If you're an
Indian you have to be real good at dying,* she would
explain over her milk and arrowroot biscuit. *Now why
is that?* I asked: I knew the answer, having played the
same games myself, but was curious to hear how she
would explain it. *Well, if you're an Indian you have to
fight bravely, see. And kill a few cowboys. But in the end
you have to get killed, the cowboys always win.* I persisted:
But Madge, why do the cowboys always win? Madge took
a long drink and sat looking at me with a white moustache. She burped and said, *Well you see Mum, the
Indians are brave and everything but backward,* and here
she was inspired. *See, they did not know how to make
guns, they only stole them from the cowboys, but the
cowboys knew how to make them.* She finished the milk
and was off again, out the door to the garden, yelling,
*Want to see me die, Mum? Watch, quick, this is how I
die.*

As well as dying, our clever Madge was good at being
a lady running a tight ship of a tea party on the lawn.
Caroline would be there in a hat of her mother's with a

white veil and a lot of blue cloth flowers, and Ellen would be there in her mother's patent-leather high heels and would later get the strap for having taken them out of their box. Our Madge was splendid in the moulting fur stole, completely bald over one shoulder, tattered of lining and smelling of camphor, that my own mother, that misty woman of gold teeth and too many wistful smiles, had left neatly packed in tissue paper in the top of the wardrobe. That stole had been the thing about her death that had made me cry, for it was in that stole, whatever the temperature of the night, that my mother had gone out with my father on their rare evenings together. She would be flushed with the excitement of it all, and anxious about her gold earrings, whose fastenings she could never quite bring herself to trust, so she had to keep plucking at her lobes all night, and would be splendid in the old stole, a farewell gift from her father in chilly Rumania. He had disapproved of his son-in-law, thought his daughter a fool for throwing herself away on him, found the idea of Australia ridiculous, but he had not wished his daughter to freeze in the barbarous land she was determined to go to. He had wished her to be protected from the snows of the new land, and he never guessed, poor man, that his daughter would never see snow again, and would never need a fur to warm her shoulders.

Mother had loved that stole, and cherished it in camphor and tissue paper, and never failed to mention her father each time she wore it. *The tears were standing in his eyes,* she told me a hundred times, *for he knew he would never see me again.* Her own eyes then never failed to fill with tears: *He was right,* she would say, and dab her eyes with her best linen hanky, a gift from me, *and Joan, it is the saddest thing, he will never know, now, how much his daughter loved her father.* Oh, fathers and their daughters, what tales of heartbreak! But that is another story.

The stole, then: Father, his cranium gleaming, would come then to take Mother in her stole off to a play she would barely follow, still after so long having not got the hang of English if it was too quick, or a dinner with business acquaintances who had to be charmed, so that poor Mother would return with a headache from smiling too much and pretending to understand more than she did. She would fling the stole off, forgetting to cry for her father, and lie in bed with a cold cloth on her forehead, and in the morning would fold the fur in its tissue again, and store it away in the top of the wardrobe before anyone was up.

That stole had seen many tears, then: those of that unknown grandfather, dead now after a lifetime of drilling molars: those of poor Mother, who had grown weepy thinking of her father, and who had wept over me and my strangeness, and who had cried stormy tears of rage, the year the moth got at the shoulder of the stole.

And now here was Madge, carrying such a burden of mixed sadnesses on her shoulders, but none of that old history was likely to bow her down. I had told her tales I had heard from my own mother, had told her of snows, wolves, pine forests howling under frosty winds, because I thought it right that some fragment of her beginnings should be known to her, that her particular kind of history should not be entirely dissolved in the new place where she was growing up. *Ah, Mum,* she whined, *not the wolves again!* and I had to admit they were pretty secondhand wolves by the time they got to her, and thin unconvincing forests, for I had no vision of wolves or snow or pine forests myself, only the stories from that poor lost mother of mine. Of that mother there were no stories I could tell, for she had done little but weep over her stole and

look confused in shops, and neither of those activities
was enough to keep the interest of our matter-of-fact
Madge for long. She pranced on the lawn and pirouetted
in her stole for Duncan's camera, like every new gen-
eration, dancing in the shadow of history's griefs.

Dear Duncan! He had taken photographs of Madge,
photographs of me, photographs of Madge and me together: he had carefully explained, and let me take photographs of him with Madge, and Madge had been allowed
to hold the precious box for long enough to capture
Duncan and me together by the front gate and on the
back lawn. But it was a different kind of day altogether
recorded here, on this last photograph, where all three
of us are showing too wild a mouthful of teeth to the
camera. There is a sort of hysteria here, and we are all
frozen, staring at the black box, holding our breaths, not
moving a muscle, as if we are afraid the black box is
not clever enough to catch us while we are moving. We
are turned to grinning stone, staring at Madge's camera
sitting on the gatepost in the front yard, ticking and
whirring all by itself, until at last it clicks and we are
released into a great deal of shouting and laughing and
all talking at once. In this photograph there is a small
dismay in Duncan's eyes, that cameras and their mysteries, which have always been his domain, are now
mysteries that Madge knows more about than he does.
She is a child no longer, and has bought a camera of her
own, a cheap little thing, but she has worked out, as
Duncan never has with all his paraphernalia, how to
make it take a photograph all by itself.

This was the day Madge, flesh of our flesh, left the
nest. She wore the red and blue striped skirt with the
rope petticoat, and the middy blouse in red that her
father had scolded her for wearing, for the way it allowed
glimpses of her flesh. *It is not right, Madge, everyone can*

269

see your stomach, he insisted, and Madge rolled her eyes
and appealed to his reason: *But Dad, that is the whole
idea, it is called middy because you can see midriff.* Madge
thought her father had become a terrible old sobersides
of a Dad, and I understood: I knew it was not in the
nature of things for the world to stand still, and history
was always out there waiting to be made not by parents,
who had had their go at it, but the children of those
parents. *They are all wearing them, love,* I tried to tell
Duncan, *it is all right,* and I remembered how my own
father had been moved to poke at my bare shoulder when
I had worn some improvised gypsy garment or other,
and remark, *If flesh is all you have, Joan, you have
nothing.*

Madge did not prance and preen and pontificate about
making history, but she was more likely to do something
about it than her mother had been. She was a bright girl,
and all the sneering of the boys at school for being too
brainy, and all the hints of the teachers that such enthusiasm for gases was not quite nice, had not so much
as scratched the shiny gloss of her love of a good problem
that needed solving.

It seemed that our Madge was not going to make any
ceremony of this moment, and not acknowledge it as
history. Everything was planned: the studies, the schol-
arship, and the room—I had seen it, Madge was kind
enough to have asked our advice, though we all knew
she did not need advice from us about her future—the
room with the view of a passionfruit vine up a drainpipe
and a small patch of sky. Madge had set all this in
motion, heaven knows how she knew so much: did I
ever know so much more than my own parents?

As I had had to stand, embarrassed, translating for
Mother at the butcher's, or try to look like a stranger to
him when Father became excited on the subject of justice

with someone at the bus stop who had just wanted to pass the time of day: as I had known enough to be ashamed of my parents, Madge knew enough to be kind where I had been callous, and knew how silent it would be when it was just Duncan and me by ourselves in the house.

Duncan sat in his armchair, the one with the worn place on the arm where his hand smoothed and stroked as he read or gazed out the window: he sat, not smoothing or stroking now, and without that faint bemused smile that meant he was at peace with his destiny: he sat listening to Madge in her room putting things in her suitcase, and opening and closing the wardrobe door.

And I: I could not sit in my armchair across from Duncan's, and watch Madge leaving home. I went into the kitchen, and was glad of the pile of dishes there, that could be scrupulously washed, and dried, and put away, and when that was done I was all for running up a batch of scones, the scones I could make now as well as anyone else, but what if Madge refused the scones and left me and Duncan with them as a steaming reminder that she was gone? So I busied myself snipping the yellowing leaves off the African violet that grew by the sink, and wiped down a cupboard door or two, and then I could not bear it any more, but had to go and watch, as Duncan was doing, while Madge packed her things, and left.

And what was it that Madge wanted to take with her from the past into the future? Our Madge was not a remarkably sentimental girl, so I was surprised to see the teddy bear that Father had given her, that she had worn as bald as the giver with the energy of her love, and the old hand-tinted photograph of somewhere in Transylvania, where Mother had told me she grew up: there was the slightly fly-specked calendar from Murchison's, with the photo of the Bridge, and the Christmas card with the

densely packed writing inside that had come from someone it made her blush to mention. I was glad about the
photograph of Transylvania, for now that I was the age
my mother had been when I had married Duncan and
gone reluctantly to share his destiny, I felt for that poor
mother of mine, who had risked everything for love, and
made such a poor bargain: although as she confessed to
me once, she would never have been able to forget my
father if she had not come with him to the new land,
so she did not regret anything.

Now it was time to say goodbye—*Just for now, Mum,
not for ever,* Madge exclaimed at my tragic face—and I
watched us all, like a spectator, as Madge left home.
There was my husband, now a bald man with a grey
moustache, and sick, and he stood in his slippers, waving
with a tired hand. *Bye-bye, Madge love,* he called, and
that Madge of ours, a thin girl full of sparks and with
more brains than was good for her, laughed and waved
back, buoyant to be leaving this house behind its hedge
and her dull parents. *Bye-bye Dad,* she called, and I was
there too, with the tea towel in my hand and the smell
of the rubber gloves around me, and she ran back up
the path to kiss me. Her cheek was hot: I felt the thrill
she felt, and remembered feeling it myself, having her
life's history still to be made, and anything possible.

It is all ahead of you, Madge, I said, and wished for
better words, but beginnings and endings bring out the
same old phrases. *Your father does not have long to go
now, and me too: it is your life now, Madge.*

But what daughter ever listens? My Madge kissed me,
and kissed her father's pale cheek: it was her own car
now beyond the hedge, ready to take her away to a future
of her own, where one day some man would pant and
exclaim over her, there would be a moment's electric
interchange, and my daughter would become in her turn

filled with the love that has no choice. We listened until
the roar of Joan's imperfect engine could no longer be
heard. Then it was just the humming of insects in the
grass, and the mad rooster out the back, crowing like a
lunatic at lunchtime, and the sighing sound of parents
stranded, washed up on the beach where the tide of life
had been, and had passed.

EPILOGUE

WHAT a big thing this business of history is, and what absurd bits and pieces make it up! Take a handful of dirt. It began as nothing much, just a few chemicals gone hard and ground up into sand, and it would have stayed that way, except that things started living and dying on it. That handful of dirt soaked up the bits of moss and grass that withered on the stem, the leaves from bushes, the branches of trees, and every kind of worm, bug, and fly that had its moment of life and then died: great scaly giants sank down on it to pant their last, birds dropped out of the sky and never rose again, every kind of furry thing hopped and ran across it and finally lay down for good. That handful of dirt rejected nothing: it soaked up the steaming urine of babies as they crawled across it laughing, and the tears of twiglike grandmothers slipping a hand under a cheekbone and waiting for the last sleep. Men and women lay down and melted into the dirt, or were put into holes and buried, or were burned away to a small heap of ash: in the end the dirt claimed them all.

It was that jumble of dead odds and ends that made that earth a fit place for men and women to sow there at last, and reap. They labored mightily, under sun and

277

rain, toiling not for that day's bread but for the future: in the lean days of winter they put seed into the ground, thinking of the feasts they would grow fat on, later: they had discovered the past and the future and could think forwards, with faith, as well as backwards. That was why their ambitions led them on and on, to greater and greater glories from that bit of dirt: they chopped and cleared, planted and harvested, herded and gathered, they picked and dug and cut, and they never stopped planning a more splendid tomorrow. They smoothed the dirt down and at last packhorses, penny-farthings, coach-and-fours, and motor cars travelled over it. They sliced the trees into planks and shaped the planks into masts, hockey sticks, church organs, books of etiquette: they invented bootees, strychnine, watered-silk, and baldness cures: oh, how pleased they were with themselves!

They planned great things, and better worlds, and went on sowing, full of hope. Centuries passed, generations of babies grew old and died, and now it is my turn: here I am, pacing down a nicely turned bit of curbing and guttering, pushing the pram containing my grandchild, and planning the stories I will tell her.

I thought my story was one the world had never heard before. I loved and was bored, I betrayed and was forgiven, I ran away and returned, and all these things appeared to be personal and highly significant history. Oh Joan, what bogus grandeur! There was not a single joy I could feel that countless Joans had not already felt, not a single mistake I could make that had not been made by some Joan before me.

There was a time when I would have raged against such a thought, or grown petulant. But now that I am such an old woman, and so many times a grandmother, I do not grieve, but grow pleased and plump at the idea. I swell like an egg: there is nothing I cannot claim as my own now, and although you may not think so to look at me, I am the entire history of the globe walking down the street.

I am weary and old now, pushing the squeaking pram and considering my life, and what a paltry thing it is. I wish I had known earlier that I was making history: if I had, I might have lived more carefully, and with my eye on the past and the future rather than on myself alone. Soon I will be part of the dirt, along with all the other things that have had their day. This hand, freckled with years of sunlight, these feet in their sensible shoes, this spine curved over the child in the pram, will be a scattering of loose bones before long, and this skull, that has been home to so many imagined lives, will become a receptacle for nothing more grand than another handful or two of dirt.

Such lugubrious thoughts should trouble me, but do not: I savor my share of life. Around me in the mauve dusk, I can hear a child screeching at the idea of bedtime, a woman singing over the dishes clattering in the sink, and someone somewhere is having a good sneeze. Long after I am dirt, there will still be such people screeching, singing, and sneezing away, and I will always be part of them. Stars blazed, protozoa coupled, apes levered themselves upright, generations of women and men lived and died, and like them all I, Joan, have made history.